K

WAⁱⁱⁱⁿ⋃

Book 3 of *The Order of the White Boar*

'Evocative and intriguing… brings the uncertain and
dangerous times after the Battle of Bosworth to life.'

Wendy Johnson, member of the Looking for Richard Project

'A wonderful work of historical fiction . . . altogether a very
enjoyable book for both children and adults.'

Isabel Green, *Ricardian Bulletin* of the Richard III Society

Also by Alex Marchant

The Order of the White Boar
The King's Man
Sons of York (pub. 2022)

Time out of Time

As editor

Grant Me the Carving of My Name
Right Trusty and Well Beloved…
(both sold in support of Scoliosis Association UK)

KING
in
WAITING

Book 3 of *The Order of the
White Boar*

Alex Marchant

Marchant Ventures

*To Alex
Loyalty binds us!
With all best
wishes
Alex*

First published 2021

Copyright © 2021 Alex Marchant

The right of Alex Marchant to be identified as the author of this work has been asserted in accordance with the Copyright, Design and Patents Act, 1988.

All rights reserved. No part of this publications may be reproduced, stored in or introduced to a retrieval system, or transmitted, in any form or by any means, electronic, mechanical, photocopying, recording or otherwise, without the prior permission of the copyright holder.

ISBN-13: 9798462198946

Cover illustration: Oliver Bennett, morevisual.me

To

Marion and John

with much love and thanks for being there!

Contents

Cast of characters

The Order of the White Boar
Matthew Wansford, a merchant's son of York
Alys Langdown, ward of Queen Elizabeth Woodville
Roger de Kynton, page to John, Earl of Lincoln
Elen, companion to Alys

In Suffolk
John de la Pole, Earl of Lincoln, son of Elizabeth, Duchess of
        Suffolk, nephew to Richard III*
Francis, Viscount Lovell, Richard III's friend and chancellor*
Lady Alice Tyrell, wife to Sir James*
Robert Mallary, gentleman of Northamptonshire*
Giles Mallary, his brother*
Master van Ghendt, an ambassador
Hugh Soulsby, a squire, nephew to Lord Walter Soulsby, cousin
        to Ralph

In Flanders
Margaret Plantagenet, dowager Duchess of Burgundy, sister to
        Richard III and Edward IV*
Edward Plantagenet, deposed King of England, son of Edward
        IV, nephew to Richard III*
Richard, Duke of York, his brother*
George, his cousin, natural son of George, Duke of Clarence

In the Channel
Captain van Hecke, Flemish master mariner
Guillaume Tournier, a Channel Islander

In Ireland
Gerald FitzGerald, Eighth Earl of Kildare*
Alison, Lady Kildare, his wife*
Sir Thomas FitzGerald, his brother*
Maurice FitzGerald, son of Sir Thomas*
Sir John Wrythe, Garter King of Arms, chief herald of England*
Sir Henry Bodrugan, a knight of Cornwall*
Berthe, Alys's maid

In the past...
Richard III, King of England*
Anne Neville, his wife*
Edward of Middleham, his son*
Edward IV, King of England, his brother*
Edmund, Earl of Rutland, his brother*
George, Duke of Clarence, his brother*
Richard, Duke of York, his father*
Richard, Earl of Warwick, his cousin, known as the Kingmaker*
Henry VI, one-time King of England, deposed by Edward IV*
Henry, Duke of Buckingham, cousin to Richard III*
Anthony Woodville, Earl Rivers, brother to Queen Elizabeth
      Woodville, uncle to Edward V*
Richard, Lord Grey, older half-brother to Edward V, younger
      son of Elizabeth Woodville by her first husband*
William, Lord Hastings, friend of Edward IV*
Master John Kendall, Richard III's secretary*

Known to history...
Henry Tudor, King of England (usurper)*
Elizabeth of York, his wife, daughter to Edward IV*
Arthur Tudor, Prince of Wales, their son*
Elizabeth Woodville, queen of Edward IV, mother of Elizabeth
      of York, later Dame Grey*
Thomas Grey, Marquess of Dorset, older half-brother to Edward
      V, eldest son of Elizabeth Woodville*
Elizabeth, Duchess of Suffolk, sister to Richard III*
Edward, Earl of Warwick, son of George, Duke of Clarence*
John of Gloucester, natural son of Richard III *
Katherine, natural daughter of Richard III*
Thomas, Lord Stanley, Earl of Derby*
Margaret, Lady Stanley, his wife, mother of Henry Tudor by her
      first husband*
Sir William Stanley, brother to Lord Thomas*
Maximilian, Archduke of Austria, son-in-law of Margaret,
      dowager Duchess of Burgundy *
John Morton, Bishop of Ely*
Sir James Tyrell, governor of Guînes*
Sir Edward Brampton, former governor of Guernsey*
Richard Harliston, former governor of Jersey*

* Historical figures

The Code of the Order of the White Boar

a b c d e f g h i j k l m n o p q r s t u v w x y z
u v w x y z a b c d e f g h i j k l m n o p q r s t Monday
r s t u v w x y z a b c d e f g h i j k l m n o p q Tuesday
o p q r s t u v w x y z a b c d e f g h i j k l m n Wednesday
l m n o p q r s t u v w x y z a b c d e f g h i j k Thursday
i j k l m n o p q r s t u v w x y z a b c d e f g h Friday
f g h i j k l m n o p q r s t u v w x y z a b c d e Saturday
c d e f g h i j k l m n o p q r s t u v w x y z a b Sunday

1

Flight

I flung myself to the ground, burying my face in the grass. I was afraid it would give me away – a pale glimmer in the darkness, if anyone glanced in my direction.

The blades of grass – dried by autumn winds, sharpened by the frost – pricked at my skin, even through the thickness of my winter hose. But I heeded them not. Above me the breeze sighed in the swaying branches of the ancient yew trees, and to one side loomed the small stone chapel, the cut flints of its walls glistening in the light of the waxing moon. If anyone cast their eyes towards me, they would see just another shadow among many in the churchyard.

I lay there, motionless, while the thudding of hooves passed in the lane, only yards away. The reek of sweat – of men and horses – drifted to me on the chill air. Harness jingled. Then horseshoes scraped on icy cobbles, a man's voice barked an order. Creaking of leather, boots thumping upon the ground.

Now the horsemen had ridden past and dismounted in the stableyard, I risked raising my head an inch or two.

The flare of brands held aloft lit up the faces of stable boys and serving men hurrying to greet the riders. The newcomers threw their reins to them and raised their voices with more demands. The servants bowed and ushered the men towards the grand house beyond. Firelight played still in the windows of its great hall. As the newcomers mounted the steps to the entrance and were swallowed up in its shadows, I lowered my head once more. I had seen enough.

Turning with difficulty, I wriggled as quietly as I

could across the spiked grass until I gained the safety of the chapel wall. I grasped its cold flints, dragged myself to my feet, then brushed my doublet free of dry clinging leaves before sprinting for the cover of the hedge, its dark line lurking far across the field. The frost-sculpted earth crackled beneath my boots.

Forcing my way through a gap in the hedge, my foot caught in a tangle of roots and I tumbled headlong. Branches of hawthorn and hazel snapped beneath my weight as I clumped to the ground. In the still silence, the sound struck my ears like cannon fire. A bird, startled from sleep, burst up from the bushes and clucked its alarm, splitting the darkness.

As I struggled back to my feet, a hand clapped over my mouth. Before I could protest, I was hauled bodily across the rutted and rocky ground along the hedge foot. I had been watched for, of course. Even had I not announced my arrival with my clumsy fall.

In the deep shade of a stately oak – its bare limbs stark against the star-studded, moonlit sky – darker shapes were mustered. Mingled together – two-legged, four-legged, men and the fidgeting bulks of horses – around a dozen shadows in all. One shape broke away, forward, towards me and my assailant. Tall, lean, the cool moonlight glinting off a hint of armour beneath his enveloping cloak, a drawn sword in his hand.

'Well?'

A single word, breathed, urgent.

'Shouldn't send a boy to do a man's job.'

The man dragging me dumped me, sprawling, on the ground. His voice, aggrieved, grumbling, but barely even a whisper.

'Matthew?' The tall figure again.

I scrambled up, my pride bruised more than my body, though my hands and knees stung where I had landed on sharp stones. Frozen crumbs of earth stuck to them still. But I did not wipe them away this time before bowing my head.

'My lord, five or six well-armed men and their captain. Their livery quartered grey and forest green. Their badge …' I hesitated, 'a large black bird. A crow perhaps? They were not expected.'

'Evidently.' My attacker snorted – the quietest such noise I had ever heard. 'Or my Lady Tyrell would not have hustled us away as she did when her men brought her warning.'

'Peace, Robert, let the boy speak.'

My questioner's voice was tense, an edge to it I had heard earlier that day. From his next question, I guessed he already knew my answer.

'Could it have been a raven?'

I thought. A raven – harbinger of death.

'Aye, my lord, it could easily.'

Did his lordship's shoulders sag a little beneath his thick cloak? It was hard to tell in the moonlight.

'Lord Soulsby's men – without a doubt.'

I flinched at the hiss of the too-familiar name.

'We must fly, my lord.' Robert's words, though still quiet, rasped the night air. 'If they find we were here, they will raise the whole country against us – claim we are all foreign spies, not good true Englishmen.' A hesitation, then he quickly twisted back to the cluster of shades beneath the oak, lifting his cap. 'Begging your pardons, of course, sirs.'

Two shadowy figures bowed in return, as his lordship muttered, 'Once Lord Soulsby himself was true to the Yorkist cause.'

'Maybe, my lord, but times have changed. And he was ever one to change with them.'

'Aye.' His lordship almost swallowed the word. But he did not move.

'Lord Francis, please.' Robert's voice, though as quiet as ever, was beseeching. 'Please, my lord, we must be away. We cannot now wait in hope that my lord of Lincoln may change his mind.'

Yet still his lordship made no move. His eyes,

reflecting the distant moon, shifted restively as though surveying the wintry landscape.

'My lord,' Robert again, 'we cannot be sure Lord Lincoln himself did not raise them. He departed long before we did.'

The reply shot back as swift and deadly as an arrow.

'Show not disrespect to your betters, Master Mallary. The Earl of Lincoln has no love of the usurper. He would not betray us.'

'Nay, my lord, I'm sure you are right. I meant no disrespect.' But the man stood his ground. 'Yet whatever the case, we cannot tarry. We must ride for the coast with all speed.'

Another harsh whisper – 'My lord!' This from among the shifting shapes beneath the oak tree. 'My lord – another rider. In the lane.'

Lord Francis spun towards the speaker.

'How many, Giles?' he hissed. 'From what direction?'

'Just one, my lord,' came the ready reply. 'Coming from the house. At speed.'

'Make ready to fly, gentlemen,' his lordship flung back. 'Robert, with me.'

As the other shadowy figures melted into the shady mass about the tree, I forced my steps after Lord Francis and Robert Mallary as they crept along the hedgeline. It was but a few yards to the gateway that gave on to the lane and as we reached it, the sound Giles's ears had picked up a moment earlier struck my own.

The steady thudding of cantering hooves upon the beaten earth of the track. A drumming that grew louder as it drew closer.

My heart pounded in my chest, the blood in my ears, in echo of the sound.

Lord Francis crouched at one side of the gateway, a dark shadow against the moonlit thread of the lane, with Robert close behind. Both held unsheathed swords, just visible in the eerie half-light. I drew my own knife and craned to see above the bare twigs of the unkempt hedge.

And what met my eyes made me call out – too loud perhaps in that quiet night.

'My lord! Hold your hand!'

At my voice, the cantering pony skittered to a halt level with the gap in the hedge. The slight figure upon it had hauled back on the reins. Swathed in a dark cloak, the hint of a white linen cap peeked from beneath the hood and pale gloves were firm upon the reins.

A cry broke and was swiftly muffled as the pony, forced back on to its haunches, reared, its forelegs flailing the air, then recovered and shied away from my voice. The rider deftly leant into its turn and spun it round a full circle before reining it back to face us. Its hooves pawed at the earth for an instant, then were still. Beyond the rider, the ghostly shape of a hound skulked among the shadows of the lane.

Lord Francis sprang forward, his hand seizing a rein.

'My lady Alys?' His tone betrayed his surprise. 'What do you here?'

'My lord, I could not stay.' The slender figure bent towards him, her words a whisper. But I was close enough to hear them, clear in the still night air.

'Not stay?' His lordship's reply was brusque. 'Why so? It was agreed with Lady Tyrell.'

'Lord Francis, those men who came. They were Lord Soulsby's men.'

'Aye. Matthew saw them. And?'

Puzzlement touched his lordship's voice. But I knew. I knew why my friend had fled the great house.

I stepped forward as she said,

'I cannot remain, my lord. Lord Soulsby —'

'Is not here himself. You will be safe at Gipping with her ladyship.'

'You cannot leave me here.' Alys's words were fierce, even in an undertone. But did a hint of desperation lurk beneath them? 'You know I cannot stay. Whether it is Lord Soulsby himself or just his men – they will report to him. You know how it will end. I will not return to London to … to marry that —'

Her voice cracked.

I reached up to touch her arm, her gloved hand clenched upon the rein, but she shook me off as though she did not know me.

'I simply cannot.'

A silence.

His lordship gazed up at her. Her face was alabaster in the moonlight – white, hard as stone – but her eyes were liquid, with a sheen of tears.

His lordship hesitated one instant only before saying,

'Very well, Alys. You may ride with us. I know … I know this marriage was not wished for by everyone. Had things been different …' He shook his head. 'I'm sure Her Grace the duchess will welcome you too. Come, Matthew, Robert – we must be away.'

He retreated to where our companions were ready, mounted, beneath the oak tree. Robert trailed in his wake.

I hesitated. My hand stole again towards Alys. This time I felt a quick squeeze of my fingers before she dropped them and took up her reins once more.

I hurried back to the shade of the massive oak, where Giles threw me the reins of my own horse, together with my bundle. I swung myself with some difficulty into the saddle. Alys at least would not slow us down on our flight to the coast. Of myself, I could not say as much.

I urged the horse to follow the rest of the party as they filed quietly into the lane. Alys took up a position alongside me without a word, and her lithe white hound drifted at our heels like a wisp of mist in the darkness.

2

Landmarks

Our progress that night was as swift as it could be in the darkness. Always we were on watch for pursuit – whether from the riders we had left behind at the great house, or from others who might be hostile or might fear danger to themselves. All around us, we imagined hidden eyes watching us from the shadows as we passed.

Much had changed since last I had travelled that way towards the coast, a little over a year before. Then I had ridden also with Alys, with her wraith-like hound, Shadow, at her horse's hooves as now, and with our old friend Roger ... and two others. Then also we had been pursued – and had suspected the mortal danger we faced if caught. Though we had not dreamed just how it would end.

I blinked away hot tears as my memory drifted back to that other dark night. To the frantic ride like this. To the fear. To the fight in the sea mist – in the alley in the port of Lowestoft, where now we were heading again. Where I had lost my best friend in all the world – bar Alys, of course.

And yet, perhaps, Murrey had been closer. She had been with me, day in, day out, and every minute of those days, for almost three years. Not just my hound. My loyal companion through all that time of my life. Then she had been struck down in an instant as she sought to defend me. Stabbed. Killed. By the cowardly, treacherous —

I tore my thoughts away. I had no wish to relive – yet again – the events of that night. To torture myself with asking if things could have been different, if I could have made different choices. If I had sought another captain, of a ship that had left earlier. If I had not delayed to tie up our first assailant, but gone to the ship with the others. If I had thus not encountered … Hugh.

Hugh Soulsby. Hearing his uncle's name this evening had brought everything back to me, alas. The stuff of my worst nightmares in the year and more since. The death of Murrey. And only days before that …

The death of my king. My sovereign master, King Richard, the third of that name. Destroyed on the field of battle – but also by treachery. At the hands of the Stanley brothers and … and Lord Soulsby and his men. That dread day would stay with me for all the years of my life.

And now the usurper Henry Tudor was king in his stead.

The names of Stanley and Soulsby were like acid on the tongues of many, I knew. May their souls be damned for ever for their treachery! Without their treasonous acts, their cowardly charge into the rear of the royal knights fighting to reach and kill Tudor, not only my king – the rightful king – but my loyal hound might still be alive now.

I dashed those memories away along with the tears that sprang again to my eyes, and gave up grateful thanks for the darkness that hid this weakness from others' sight. Even from Alys, who rode always by my side, her spirited pony held back to keep pace with my old hack. Far better it would be to dwell on happier events.

Such as meeting again with Alys at Gipping Hall. And with Roger and with Elen. These past two days had brought we friends back together at last. And before that I had enjoyed long days of happy anticipation – of hope for what the future might bring.

We passed now the first of many landmarks I recalled from our long ride yesterday from the coast – an ancient church with crumbling spire stark against the pearly sheen of the moonlight.

And I remembered …

Remembered standing on the harbour wall in the small Low Countries port. Breathing in the good salt smell. Watching the soft swell of the sea and the stream of milk-white moonlight stretching across the inky water, away towards the horizon. From time to time feeling the light touch of the spray pepper my face as the breeze caught a stray wave and dashed it against the old stone bulwark. And seeing lights, far off, in the distance.

Far off, in the dark grey distance, across the shining moonlit waves.

Or did I? Did I really see those lights of home? Of faraway England?

Or was it just the dull, heavy mixture of tiredness and longing that had hung about me all these months?

Longing to be with my friends again, my family. To know if they were safe. To find out what was happening in troubled, turbulent England. To see for myself, not rely on scant news from official letters – letters to those I now lived amongst, only once or twice letters to me from my friends. Reassuring words came sometimes – but hemmed in all around by news that was not so comforting. News of rebellions, uprisings against the new king, attempts on his life, executions in reprisal, heavy fines for those who might think to assist.

Tumultuous times.

Times of fear, uncertainty, unknown futures. Not knowing who or when to trust – or, sometimes, even how. Even the new king, King Henry, the seventh of that name – now crowned, anointed, married to his Yorkist bride, father already to a new dynastic heir – he knew not whom he could trust, it was said. So he cajoled, bribed, threatened his way around the land.

And some welcomed his rule, some accepted it as they could see no alternative. Some bided their time ...

Troubling, troubled times.

Was it all this that tricked my eye into seeing those distant lamps? The longing to be there? The sickness to be at home?

The feeling speared through me again.

From high above drifted down the lonesome honking of geese, flying west, towards my homeland.

Yet could it ever be my home again? I could not fly, like those geese, far above the eyes of Tudor's wakeful watchers on the coast – to alight far inland, unseen, unsuspected, on fields of winter wheat, shooting green from the frozen ground, as the geese did every year. Any return for us would always be a risk. Not only from Tudor's agents, but from any who might betray us – any who might seek to profit from telling of our arrival.

Was it a risk we would always face?

'Boy!'

The sailor's shout had broken through my thoughts. In the guttural Flemish tongue I knew so well now from my many months here.

'Get yourself on board, boy, if you're coming with us.'

I hurried on to the ship, the gangplank swaying a little above the gentle rolling of the waves.

Looking down. Flotsam eddying on the moonlit foam.

Me? Tossed one way, then another.

What would I find when I returned to my homeland?

The old stone windmill next to the road glimpsed again as our party flashed by. Its broken sail still rotated sadly, catching, throwing off the light from the setting moon.

And I remembered …

Arrival at the stableyard, the grand entrance, the great hall of Gipping.

My two companions – emissaries from Burgundy – greeted cordially by Lady Tyrell before the blazing fire. Their courteous bows deep before her, the rich fabrics of their garments reflecting the bright hues of the flames, their doffed caps brushing the grey stone flags of the floor.

Memories of a year before flooding my head as I hung back.

Memories of two boys – faced across this same stone-flagged expanse. Their shadowed eyes. Their suspicion.

Murrey begging to go to them – dancing her pirouette, playing dead at a command, taking her tidbit reward with delicate teeth.

The taller boy – Edward, he who would now be king – haughty, unwelcoming.

Young Richard, his brother, cowed by the news I brought.

'Henry Tudor won't restore you to your throne. Henry Tudor won't let you live. You must flee – with us – to Flanders – to your aunt, grand duchess there.'

But yesterday it had been Alys gliding across those grey flagstones with Shadow bounding at her heels, Alys flinging herself into my unready arms. Lady Tyrell disapproving. A lady wouldn't ...

'Matt – how wonderful to see you! How lonely it has been here!' A turn, a bobbed curtscy to her ladyship. 'Though Lady Tyrell has been so good to me, so kind. Almost like a mother.'

The faintest smile curving her ladyship's thin lips as she turned back to her Burgundian guests, inviting them to sit close to the fire. Waving forward servants with spiced wine and platters of food to warm them further.

Alys drawing me into a side chamber, away from the official business in the hall. Pouring out her news. From all those months we had been apart, since she had returned to England.

Not to her home. Like me she had no real home now. Not the long-known comfort of Middleham Castle, its familiar routine, people and places from before Duke Richard became king. Not the rich formality of the court when Duchess Anne was newly queen. Not the intimate, young-girls-together of her life in Lady Elizabeth's household.

That last no longer existed – not since Elizabeth herself had become queen in her aunt Anne's place ... or at least, since she had become wife to Henry Tudor and given birth to his child.

'Elen came too, a few weeks ago, so we have been dull here together,' she said, rounding off her news. 'Elizabeth sent her to Lady Tyrell to get her away from court for a while. Since the birth of her son, all her ladies have been arranged for her by Lady Stanley, and the old witch fears Elen and Elizabeth's other ladies are not to be trusted.'

She made a face. I had missed that – her grimaces – so unladylike.

'Elen laughed it off, but I know that she was hurt. The notion that the usurper's mother should suspect anyone, let alone Elen, would harm her precious grandson!'

Yet perhaps Tudor and his mother had cause to be worried.

Many whispered and questioned, shocked that he had not yet crowned the Lady Elizabeth queen after all these months – despite marrying her, despite the birth of an heir, despite reversing the law that had proclaimed her illegitimate – the law that three long years before had made Duke Richard king. Whatever her changing legal position, her royal blood meant she stood far above Tudor's own non-royal origins. He might have won his throne by conquest, in battle, but the whole country knew he would only keep it – if at all – with the aid of his Yorkist bride. Tudor had promised to unite the houses of Lancaster and York by his marriage – and not to make her queen would be a slight to his new allies. Why would he risk offending them?

But my thoughts then were all for our other friends.

'Whatever the reason for it, I'm glad Elen is here too. I look forward to seeing her again. It's been such a long time.'

A very long time, more than a year – since we had parted in London.

Elen standing, waving farewell, on the steps of Master Ashley's townhouse. Alongside her, my old fellow-apprentice, Simon. Together supporting Mistress Ashley, her face bruised and bloody from the blows of Tudor's agents. Master and Mistress Ashley – whom I had met often in our joint exile in Flanders ...

I had forced my mind away from that long year of banishment.

'And Roger?'

I had had little enough news from Roger himself. As ever. He was still no letter-writer. He still had more valuable uses for his time.

'Roger will be here soon. Tomorrow perhaps. And then the Order of the White Boar shall be together again.'

Alys's face had shone with pleasure – pleasure I had also not seen in so very long. Not since ... when? Before our parting in the Low Countries, when first Roger, then she, had returned to England to their different households? Before that fateful day in August? No, perhaps even longer ago – before the death of poor little Ed, far from us, far even from his parents, on that cold spring day in Middleham.

Not all the Order would be here.

But Alys's next words deflected me from my sadness, guiding me back to the present.

'He will be attending with the Earl of Lincoln, whenever he arrives. He sent me a note from Wingfield – just a line or two, of course. He says he has been doing his best to persuade Lord Lincoln to our cause. Not that he thinks it is his place, or that he can do much good.'

Then Elen, entering the room, demure as always, quiet and graceful in movement and speech. As far from Alys's quick vivacity as it was possible to be. Her surprise, then dawning smile, at my clumsy, impulsive embrace.

The warmth rising in my cheeks at her soft words of greeting – of praise at my growth in height (though it was still not great) and my gentlemanly ways. I was, of course, a lowly apprentice no more, but member of the household of the magnificent dowager Duchess of Burgundy. Yet, for all my new-found status, I did not feel I filled those shoes – not the well-crafted Italian leather boots I wore to go with my fine ducal livery.

A winding of the river I remembered from our ride yesterday. Clattering over the craggy stone bridge.

Casting worried glances to left, to right, back over our shoulders.

Would any hear us?

No lights kindled in the cottages.

Perhaps we would be safe a little longer. But back away from the road, back to the paths through the pitch-dark water meadows.

Away from any prying eyes.

And I remembered …

Roger's arrival in the morning, accompanying the lordly Earl of Lincoln. Attired as a squire. (Envious? Not I, not at all.) One of two or three companions only.

His easy grin and wink as he caught my eye, though he stayed in the background, ready to serve his master at a word.

John of Lincoln. Eldest son of the Duke of Suffolk and his wife – she who was sister to two kings, Edward and my liege lord, Richard. And at first sight my lord of Lincoln brought to my mind more his older uncle.

Tall and well-built, though with the leanness of youth. Fair of hair and face. An easy, stately manner, though now his blue eyes were home to shadows.

Then, though I had not known he was there, Viscount Francis Lovell had entered the hall, attended by two companions.

Greatest friend of my master, King Richard, and with him almost till the end – till swept away by the tide of battle.

He and the earl met and shook hands on easy terms, though son of a duke stands higher than a viscount. But these two men knew each other of old, I knew. Lord Francis was once the ward of Earl John's father – and they were united in their devotion to the Yorkist cause.

I had not seen Lord Francis since we had swapped horses and more in the aftermath of battle. When, haunted by all we had witnessed or been through, we had parted, full of sorrow, he to sanctuary at Colchester to tend his battle wounds, me to London, to Master Ashley to deliver a message – and thence I knew not where.

He nodded his head to me as he took Earl John's arm to lead him to a private chamber. He recognized me.

And later, when he took a chance to speak to me alone after dinner in the great hall, he honoured me by recalling what I had done. With my friends, of course – with what was then left of the Order.

Alys and Roger and me – and Murrey.

Taking the young princes that were – and were again now, legitimized with their sister – to their aunt Margaret – grand Duchess of Burgundy. Another sister to those two kings. Another loyal supporter of the Yorkist cause.

And there and then I unbuckled from my waist – not his swordbelt, that was long gone, used to bind Hugh Soulsby as he lay at my mercy – but his finely tooled scabbard. And within it —

Lord Francis unsheathed his sword reverently. It shone clean and sweet in the glow of the roaring log fire. Its hilt plain, bound with leather.

He kissed it as he had that day on which he gave it to me. And glanced at me.

Memories crowded his hazel eyes, mingling with the colours of a dying autumn day.

'I thank you for keeping it safe, Matthew. And for returning it to me. It – we – still have much work to do.'

The country was flattening now, marshy reed beds, as the river meandered towards the sea.

Back to the road, lest we lose ourselves in the wetlands, with their ditches and bogs, and swirling flocks of waterfowl, wheeling, restless in the freezing night air.

A risk – but surely we were almost safe at the port? If pursuit there were, would it not have caught us by now?

Had Lady Tyrell persuaded Lord Soulsby's men that whatever news they had heard about Yorkist rebels lurking in this part of Suffolk was false?

And I remembered ...

3

My Lord of Lincoln

Being ushered into Lady Tyrell's private chamber.

Bright tapestries adorning the walls, bright fire in the enormous hearth. The light of the westering sun filtering through the mullioned windows, the clear, pale, late autumn sky forecasting a frosty night.

Newly built apartments, light and airy. A modern great house, reward for faithful service to two kings.

Sir James Tyrell – away still in Calais – serving his third king. Faithfully? Did he know what his wife now did? That she conspired with rebels?

Or one rebel at least. Would there be another?

Lord Francis had waved me forwards. I bowed to him and to my lord of Lincoln.

The earl's eyes were shadowed still, his face serious, a frown line growing on his brow despite his youth. Twenty-four or twenty-five perhaps, a few years younger than Lord Francis. Not many years older than me, it was true. But his station in life so far above mine.

His gaze held me for some moments, before he motioned to me to be seated. A stool was drawn up before the fire – in front of his own and Lord Francis's richly carved chairs.

I felt myself transported back through the years to those evenings spent with Duke Richard at Middleham Castle and elsewhere. But here was no flagon of wine, no tray of sweetmeats, no lute in my hands to while away the time in pleasant song. Yet when he spoke, there was something about Earl John's voice, his manner, that recalled both his uncles – both his dead, lamented royal uncles.

'Francis—' he stopped, correcting himself, 'I mean, Lord Lovell here, tells me that you served my uncle,

King Richard, well – both as his page and ... afterwards.'

I bent my head. My eyes stung of a sudden and I hoped my show of deference would conceal it.

'And that now you serve his nephew, my cousin Edward, son of my uncle Edward, who was king before. That you fled England with him more than a year ago on my uncle Richard's orders.'

There was a question in his voice that was so like those of his uncles.

Lord Francis had not told me what to say, simply that he would bring me to meet with the earl and that I must tell him the truth. The whole truth.

'Aye, my lord. I serve him gladly. As my master King Richard instructed me.'

'I see you still wear my uncle's badge.'

The earl had spotted the silver boar that nestled just beneath the collar of my doublet – as always, and often to Edward's annoyance.

His sharp eyes returned to my face.

'Where is my cousin now?'

I hesitated.

Yet this man, as he said, was family to King Richard, to Edward himself. Lord Francis trusted him. Roger had told me in the time we had snatched together that he was a good master, and in unguarded, private moments, often spoke of the calamity that had befallen England with the usurper's victory – though at court he was careful to whom he spoke such words. And Lord Francis had instructed me.

I must overcome my natural caution.

'He is residing in Flanders, my lord – at present in Mechelen. With his aunt, the dowager Duchess of Burgundy.'

Earl John was thoughtful a moment.

'My aunt too. Margaret. Who swore never to rest until Henry Tudor is defeated.'

'Aye, my lord. She will do all she can to restore her family to the throne.'

She had said as much even to me. As she asked me to undertake this mission on her behalf. To brave a crossing of the northern sea in this late season. To risk a meeting with a possible rebel. To serve my new master, Edward, to the best of my ability.

'All she can? Would that include putting up an impostor in hopes that Yorkists will flock to his cause?'

His words struck me to momentary silence. This I had not expected. That I would have to vouch for Edward I had understood. Not that the earl's suspicions would run so deep.

I swallowed hard to recover my voice, to protest.

'My lord, no! Why would she do that? An impostor? How would that return her family, the mighty Plantagenets – your family too – to their rightful place? No, my lord, Edward is no impostor.'

'It is what the rumours say around London and at court. That the boy Edward and his brother died at my uncle Richard's hands. That my uncle did away with them so he could be king. That this boy at my aunt's court – oh, yes, Tudor knows of him – he has spies in many places –' Earl John's eyes were hooded, his voice tense, 'they say that this boy is a low-born child, being tutored in the ways of princes to trick the unwary into mounting rebellion against the new king.'

My heart hammered in my chest at his words, and the blood rushed to my face.

Once before, three years ago, during the great rebellion against King Richard, I had heard those rumours. The slanders against King Richard – accusations of murder. Spoken with immense relish by one Hugh Soulsby. To hear the same from one so close to King Richard – his kin even – was a shock to me.

Yet I also I recalled my own reception of the lies – and how the doubt kindled by them had lingered within me for almost two years.

I glanced at Lord Francis.

His face showed no expression, though his eyes

had narrowed at the words. Now he nodded at me, the movement so faint I scarcely saw it.

I mastered myself with some difficulty.

'My lord, I beg you, give no credence to such rumours. I am proof that Edward Plantagenet, son of our good King Edward the Fourth, still lives.'

And I told Earl John my story. As briefly as I could.

From my arrival at Middleham Castle to serve his uncle, to my Christmas visit to Westminster when I first met young Prince Edward, to our encounter at Stony Stratford some weeks later when he was newly king. To our meeting again in this very house, and our desperate race together to the coast where he was so badly wounded by Ralph Soulsby – and our flight across the sea to Friesland, and from there the hard, dangerous journey to friendly Flanders ... uncertain whether he would live or die.

A pause hung between us before the earl spoke again.

'And live he did?'

'Aye, my lord – though he was near death for many weeks. But live he does. And he is fit and well enough to seek to claim his throne, now—' my words faltered, aware what I was saying, but I carried on, 'now that he has been made legitimate once more – and is therefore rightful heir.'

The earl was silent again. Perhaps his thoughts echoed mine. Without the law that Henry Tudor had used to legitimize Lady Elizabeth, he himself, John de la Pole, Earl of Lincoln, was closest heir to the throne of England. Two years ago, everyone throughout the realm had been certain King Richard was preparing this nephew to take the reins of power. He had no other heir then – not after the sad death of his own son, little Ed.

Lord Francis spoke now for the first time since I had entered the room.

'You have a token of good faith to show my lord of Lincoln, Matthew?'

I was startled out of my memories.

'Indeed, my lord.'

I stood and rummaged in the pouch at my belt, bringing out a small but weighty blue velvet bag with a drawstring of golden cord. Kneeling before the earl, I offered it up to him.

He loosened the cord and shook the contents out on to his hand. A heavy chain of gold links, splintering the firelight into buttery golden sparks.

Then a gasp slipped from his lips. Turning its coils over and about with his fingers, he had found the intended token.

The chain of solid gold – itself a precious thing beyond the wealth of most men – was held together by a clasp of the finest workmanship. The rays of a sun in splendour – King Edward's own symbol – flickered to the eye as though alive, and at their very centre was an enormous blood ruby. Together the stone and setting shone like the brilliance of the midsummer noonday sun – here out-glorying the fire in the magnificent hearth. It was craftsmanship the like of which I had never seen before – and nor, it seemed, had Earl John.

A moment passed before he could speak.

'I have heard of this jewel. It was made for my uncle Edward to celebrate his victories at the battles of Barnet and Tewkesbury – when he reclaimed his throne. And I heard he gave it to ...' he raised his eyes to mine, 'to his son that last Christmastide before he died.'

I had seen it myself for the first time then. Adorning young Edward's neck on that Twelfth Night we had spent together when it was newly his – when we had feasted, danced, watched the mummers. I had not known its history then. But I had learnt it in the weeks and months following our arrival in Flanders. As Edward had recovered from his wound and gradually regained his strength. It was, he told me bitterly, one of the few things his uncle Richard had left to him when Parliament declared him illegitimate. He said he valued it for the memory of his father – but he would rather have been left his father's name.

I shifted, uncomfortable at the memory. The earl was still watching me. The line upon his forehead had deepened – or was it the effect of the firelight?

'It is indeed a precious jewel. And not one to be entrusted lightly to ... What are you exactly, Master Wansford? Lord Francis told me you were once page to my uncle Richard, but now ...?'

What was I now? Did I even know myself?

'I am King Edward's man now, sir. His scribe, his emissary today. His servant, I suppose.'

Also his confidant? Maybe. He had often confided in me – since I had been in his service. Since our paths had crossed one more time. And yet ...

The earl handed me back the chain, safe once again in its rich velvet resting place. I stowed it away in my pouch as before and drew out something else. A folded square of parchment, sealed with wax, stamped with a new carved seal depicting the arms of the King of England.

'And, my lord, His Grace King Edward the Fifth sends you by me a letter.'

Edward had insisted I use those exact words. His Grace King Edward. If I should have the chance to address Earl John myself.

The earl accepted the letter, glancing up at me once more, then cracking open the seal. He read it slowly – or perhaps more than once, I could not tell. I waited patiently, knowing it was not my place to speak before I was spoken to. Hunger grew in Lord Francis's eyes as he watched, and when Earl John at last offered him the parchment, he almost snatched it from his hand.

As Lord Francis read, the earl remained silent, gazing into the depths of the fire, deep in his thoughts. His lordship finished with a sigh and returned the letter to the other man. The trace of a smile was upon his lips. It was a good letter, I knew, and his reaction told me his lordship believed so too.

'And you are sure this boy is Edward?'

The earl's question broke the silence. His eyes were now fixed again on me.

'Yes, my lord. Certain.'

'And how old is he?'

I made swift calculations in my head. If last Sunday was the feast day of ...

'Sixteen, my lord.' Just a few months younger than me. 'Almost a man.'

'Indeed. Of an age fit to rule – with the good guidance of counsellors. And he can handle a weapon? In anger, I mean, not just in the training yard.'

My mind flew back to that dark, foggy night at Lowestoft. When Edward and young Richard together had so nearly bested our first assailant, Ralph Soulsby, though still just boys. And then to my image of him as I left his aunt's palace at Mechelen. Passing me back the letter I had penned to his dictation, after signing and sealing it with the great seal the duchess had had made. Standing straight and tall, clad in the finest Burgundian fashions.

Every inch his father's son.

'Yes, my lord. I witnessed it for myself before his unlucky wound. And he is a superb rider – he often competes in the duchess's tiltyard.'

'So, a young man fit to lead an army perhaps.'

Lord Francis's eyes flashed to mine and narrowed again. My heart sank within me. Had I taken a misstep? Uttered a wrong word?

Perhaps Lord Francis saw the panic on my face. His head shook minutely, almost unseen.

The earl did not see it at any rate. He was staring again at the flickering flames in the grate. Some moments passed before he roused himself, and his words were again directed to his friend.

'I have thought long and hard on this as you must know, Francis – while you were in sanctuary and then

33

abroad in the country. And I have spoken with my mother.'

'Not, I hope, your father,' Lord Francis said. 'The word is he has sworn his oath of loyalty to Tudor.'

'No, not with my father. Though he has made his views known to me. As has the —' the earl's grimace told us of whom he was to speak – 'as has Henry Tudor. He has offered me much to gain my loyalty – lands, riches, a place at his side. But be assured my decision today is not swayed by that. I believe this lad when he says my cousin Edward has returned from the dead. And I believe him now to be the true King of England. But now, after more than a year, I cannot agree to join him and lead an army for him.'

It was as though all the lights in the room had been doused. Lord Francis's breath – held from the moment the earl had opened his mouth to speak – was released in the faintest of hisses. The earl did not – or chose not to – notice as he went on.

'For all his faults – and they are many – Tudor has ruled now for more than a year. The country is at peace again —'

'You call it peace?' Lord Francis asked. 'With all the uprisings against him? Rebellions brewing in many towns?'

'Perhaps peace is not quite the right word.' Earl John's reply was calm, a small smile even playing about his lips. 'There have been many uprisings, it's true, even though Tudor has tried to downplay them. The Harringtons, old Bodrugan in the west country, the Staffords. I heard you had a hand in that, Francis. And you yourself came close to killing Tudor at York in the spring.'

This was news to me, but I must wait for details until I met my friends again.

His lordship nodded, a curt gesture.

'If more men could have been persuaded to ignore his threats and his bribes, perhaps I would have had more success.'

Earl John paused, as though meditating, before continuing.

'I know that when my uncle Richard was king, we had real peace – as we had for a dozen years before that under my uncle Edward. Save, of course, for the unrest stirred up by Tudor's mother, which my foolish cousin Buckingham was gulled into joining.'

'That was supported by few enough people here in England,' said Lord Francis. 'Mostly malcontents who threw in their lot with Lancastrians and Woodvilles – hoping to gain their favour or keep their own corrupt appointments.'

'Aye, that's true enough. And my uncle Richard soon restored the peace, and all was well for almost two years. But he used to say to me, while Tudor remains on the continent – a pretender, a tool to be used by foreign princes for their own ends – peace will always be fleeting. Which is why perhaps he was so keen to face Tudor – to rid himself of that threat.'

Another moment passed before Earl John, looking no longer at Lord Francis, let alone me, resumed.

'Young Edward now is another such pretender. With my aunt of Burgundy, and maybe Duke Maximilian, ready to provide troops and money for his attempt to take the English throne. Is he also a tool for them to use against England? For their own purposes?'

Lord Francis went to speak, but the earl raised his hand to forestall him.

'If England is at peace within itself, it can turn its attentions outwards. You know that, Francis. Perhaps it would seek to retake its old lands in France. Perhaps unite with – who? Spain? Portugal? – against its enemies. Always there is strife among the princes across the sea. I do not wish to be a tool of such stratagems, even for my respected aunt. Even with a chance to restore my family line to the throne.'

Another pause.

All he said sank but slowly into my brain, but

Lord Francis knew the import of his words. His fist was clenched tight upon the pommel of his sword, the firelight dancing gold across the white knuckles, but he did not speak.

'So,' the earl went on, slowly, as though choosing his words with care, 'although I have spoken in support of rebellion before – even given money to those who opposed Tudor – now ... now I do not believe my place is to aid another pretender – however rightful his claim. Not if it will unsettle England again. My cousin Elizabeth – his sister – has given birth to an heir for Tudor. Young Prince Arthur. There is a chance that this union of York and Tudor's Lancastrian line – however tenuous that may be – may yet bring real peace to England.'

Silence followed, a tense silence, before Lord Francis said, 'Is that truly what you believe? Or has your father —'

'My father has other sons,' the earl cut in. 'Any of my brothers could be earl in my place. Gain his favour and that of Tudor if I throw my life away. And, yes, since my uncle Richard's death my father has urged me not to involve myself. But Tudor, of course, has kept me close to him, at court and on his progresses round the country. I have seen the usurper up close. While I do not like him as a man, perhaps he also, with the guidance of good counsellors, could learn to govern well.'

'Good counsellors?' Lord Francis shot back. 'Has he surrounded himself with them yet? He has Morton and Stanley by his side.'

'Perhaps not, but he may learn. And learn that a country is not to be ruled by a mailed fist alone.'

'Then you prefer to throw in your lot with him?'

'Francis,' the earl frowned, showing emotion for the first time since he'd begun to speak, 'it is not that I prefer it, believe me. It is just that – of two evils facing our beloved country – I feel that perhaps continuing as we are now holds more promise than to plunge it into needless strife again. Had you but come a year ago, when there was still appetite for rebellion …'

He shook his head, the line in his brow deepening as though he was weary of the conversation. Lord Francis, though, was not ready to let it end.

'Yet with Edward on the throne – a Yorkist king – guided by right-thinking men … yourself amongst them, your father —'

'If Edward regains his throne, I will serve him. As well as I am able. You may take him that promise from me. But ... but not to wage war against our own people. Not to lead his army. And from what you say –' his eyes flicked my way, 'he is capable of leading that army himself, should he choose to raise it.'

A hollow opened inside my stomach at his words, his glance. I had failed in my mission.

Across the flat landscape, one, two, more lights grew in the distance.

Lowestoft.

Not far now.

We were sure to make it back to our ship, waiting patiently in the harbour to take its passengers back to Flanders.

But how many passengers?

It would be one, at least, fewer than we had hoped.

4

The Order Reunited

'Well, that went well!'

Sarcasm had dripped from Alys's words, like oil from a fractured lamp.

Roger had said nothing, only smiled his most sympathetic smile.

Elen continued with her sewing, her head bowed.

'It wasn't my fault,' I had protested. 'Lord Francis said I mustn't blame myself. He said I did my job as well as I could. That he believed Earl John had arrived with his mind made up – whatever I or he might say.'

Alys relented.

'I'm sorry, Matt. I'm sure Lord Francis is right. It's just that ... well, all our hopes were riding on this meeting. Lady Tyrell's, Lord Francis's, Duchess Margaret, the Duchess of Suffolk – all those Yorkists across the country with whom they've been in touch.'

'But all may not be lost,' Roger spoke up. 'If Lord Francis plans to stay here a day or two more, it may yet be that Earl John will change his mind.'

'Now he's heard everything, you mean?' asked Alys.

'And when he has spoken again to his lady mother. She can be very persuasive, I'm told. And her house at Wingfield is not so far from Gipping. She could easily send word to Lord Francis if the earl's decision changes.'

'If she has the chance,' I had said grimly. 'Lord Francis did tell Earl John he would wait in case he has a further message from him. But then the earl said he only had permission to be a few days away from court – to visit his mother as she was ill. Of course, she is not ill – and Tudor may know that.'

'And he may suspect it was a ruse?' asked Alys, her green eyes wide.

'Aye. Lord Francis was shocked. He said, "You asked the usurper's permission?" Then, "I have not kept myself free all these months just to be betrayed by the misstep of a callow youth."'

'He called the earl that?'

Roger laughed. 'I've heard his father call him that often. Worse than that. It won't have pleased him.'

'It didn't. His cheeks flamed red – and not just in the heat from the fire. Lord Francis apologized swiftly, blamed his disappointment, and they parted as friends, shaking hands and embracing.'

'But what if the earl had been watched and then followed here?' said Alys.

'Lord Francis spoke to Lady Tyrell afterwards. She ordered more men out to watch and to check the lanes hereabouts.' I did my best to reassure her – and myself.

'Well,' said Roger, 'it seems the reunion of the Order will be short lived. Earl John has sent word that we ride back to Wingfield soon, though darkness is falling.'

'You must go with him? It's been so long since we've seen you, and we've had so little time today.'

'I'm afraid so, Matt. My father says I must be loyal in my service to the earl. Not vanish again like last year.'

'Did you tell him where you were?'

'No, of course not!' It was Roger's turn to be shocked. 'My father is loyal to the Yorkist cause, but he prefers not to get involved in politics. Just give him a sword and tell him who to fight, and then he's happy.'

'Yet he didn't fight with King Richard,' said Alys.

'That wasn't his fault,' insisted Roger. 'He was on the south coast, watching for the invasion. When the king sent out the call to muster in Leicester, he was told to remain in case the French sent further ships. Otherwise he would have ridden north with Lord Francis, I'm sure of it.'

He half-grinned, apologetically. 'Of course, at all times he would rather be hunting.'

'Like father like son.'

'Of course.' Roger's smile broadened. 'And you know, there is some fine hunting around Wingfield. I hope Earl John will take a little time to think over his decision before he returns to court in London.'

Soon we were chatting again about anything and everything as we had long been wont to do, as though it had not been so many months since we had met. Even Elen joined in, telling us of her life with the Lady Elizabeth, of Simon (apprenticed now to Master Caxton to continue learning the printer's trade), and then of how she longed to be with Alys again.

'I don't think we have ever been so long apart, not since we were first together at Middleham,' she had said, her eyes lowering again to her needlework, but not before I had spotted an unnatural brilliance in their black depths. Was she close to tears?

'Then we must enjoy our time together while you are still here,' Alys had said, oblivious to her emotion – or choosing not to see it. 'Once you are recalled to serve Elizabeth, you must forget me. If Dame Grey,' she still used this name for her guardian, the old queen, 'finds that I am in England again, you know what will happen. Better that Elizabeth doesn't know and then she cannot let slip to her mother.'

'And you would rather hide out here than be at court?' asked Roger.

'If I must stay in England.' Alys shot me a quick look. 'Lady Tyrell does me the kindness to feed and clothe me, though I add nothing to her household.'

I knew what her look meant. Alys had been sent back to England in the early weeks after Tudor's victory, when all was unsettled – uprisings common, political alliances shifting, old enemies uniting in common cause against Tudor, then breaking apart again, swords drawn. When rumours even floated about, like scum on a stagnant pool, that Tudor himself had died of plague. Duchess Margaret had thought, perhaps, an alliance might be possible – with the old queen, her eldest son the Marquess of Dorset, Lords Surrey and Lincoln, Lord Soulsby even? Alys and her fortune would always be a valuable pawn in any shifting game of diplomatic chess to be played in the twilight of such uncertain days.

But no. It had been too early to know whether Edward would survive, and his brother Richard, at only twelve, was too young to risk on such a gamble. Their mother, old Queen Elizabeth, was told they were alive, but not of their whereabouts, in case word reached Tudor himself. And so, offered only an heiress and an unlikely patchwork of alliances – and no surety of any son to place upon the throne – she chose to see her daughter become the usurper's wife and likely also, eventually, Queen of England – rather than hazard that possibility on the throw of the dice of rebellion.

And Alys herself had been forgotten, left alone in now hostile England. So good Lady Tyrell, her friend from her early days at court and shelterer of the boys who had been princes, had offered her a home. The dust had settled on the new regime, and when the Soulsbys – in favour with it, of course, after their actions on the battlefield – sought once more for the heiress and fortune they had been promised years before ... she was nowhere to be found.

'Your own money would pay for food and clothes, the finest you could wish for,' said Roger. 'You'd want for nothing with your fortune.'

'Oh, Roger, have you forgotten? Dame Grey controls it. Until I marry, at least. Then my husband will. And he ...'

A grimace fleeted across her face, reminding me of the difficulty she faced.

'Dame Grey still wishes you to marry Ralph Soulsby?'

'It's said no other family will give their daughter to him since his injury, so his father would be happy to have him marry even me. Me and my fortune, of course.'

My mind went back to the only time I had seen Ralph – on that fateful evening in Lowestoft, fighting and wounding Edward, then himself being felled by Richard, Roger and myself, aided by two excitable hounds. The sickening thud as his head hit the house front still reverberated in my memory – lodged alongside the stickiness and sweet smell of the blood seeping on to my hands as I tied him up.

'They say he acts as though he is little more than a child now,' came Elen's quiet voice. 'He is never seen at court – nor indeed by any who visit his father's house. They say he is hidden away when there are callers.'

'There! I feel sorry for him now. But remember him also as he was before. Would you have me wed such a man so as to keep you company, Elen? And Roger – so I can buy my own clothes?'

They had no answer to that. Even Roger lowered his eyes to avoid her defiant gaze, and he looked almost relieved when a servant arrived to summon him to attend Earl John.

I clasped hands with him.

'I'm sorry you must leave so soon.'

'I must, Matt. Earl John is my liege lord now. I will write, though – whenever I can.'

I knew Roger's promises about letters of old. I had scarcely ever received one from him – and those just a few lines long, mostly about hounds and hawks and hunting. But I couldn't argue, not now.

Instead, I smiled.

'Of course. I will await your letters with eagerness.'

Alys's eyebrow arched, but she said nothing.

Roger's face was split by a grin. Then a frown elbowed it aside.

'Of course, it may be difficult – what with you being in Flanders. And there being no friendship between Duchess Margaret and the king.'

'The king?' Alys's voice was sharp. 'Don't call him that. He's plain Henry Tudor. The real king – well, the real king now is over there in Flanders. Don't forget that.'

'No, of course not. I had not forgotten. It's just that —' Roger bowed, his movement awkward, before he caught her hand and pressed it to his lips, then to his heart.

'I must bid you farewell, my lady. Who knows when we will meet again? But I shall ever carry your image deep within my heart.'

His gallantries whisked me back to our early days of friendship at Middleham, when he and Alys had often acted out scenes from romance books – of courtly language with elaborate flattery, as chivalrous knights swore undying love to beautiful damsels. Then we had all been just children, playing parts. Now, though ...

Alys laughed, pushing him away with her other hand. She had clearly forgiven him his error.

'Farewell, Sir Knight. And may our good Lord in Heaven keep you safe in all your endeavours.'

Our final farewells had been swift, for Earl John wished to depart before the evening darkness was too far advanced. After we had waved Roger off from the stableyard, we trailed back to the great hall, each in our own thoughts. How long would it be before we met him again? And would the earl change his mind?

Lord Francis, Lady Tyrell and the two gentlemen who had accompanied me from Burgundy were speaking together as we entered. Lurking in the shadows away from the fire were two other men, those who had first arrived in company with Lord Francis.

Both were dark of hair, blue of eye and similar in looks, though one was older by some years and shorter and stockier than the other. I had been seated next to the younger at dinner, and from him learned that he was Giles Mallary, here with his brother Robert – both gentlemen from Northamptonshire who had aided Lord Francis in his secret travels about the land this past year. Giles nodded in recognition to me now, before resuming his whispered conversation with his brother.

Before Alys, Elen and I had a chance to settle into talk ourselves or escape to a more private place, Lady Tyrell retreated to her own chamber, and after a brief discussion, four of the gentlemen scattered through other doorways, each taking with him a flaming brand from the holders affixed to the walls. Lord Francis lingered behind, one hand resting on the hilt of his sword as he gazed about the great hall, lit now only by the flames leaping on the hearth.

Spotting us hesitating near the main doorway, he came over. After a courteous nod to Alys and Elen, he spoke to me, although, with his eyes still flickering around the dancing shadows of the hall, his thoughts appeared elsewhere.

'Matthew, I had hoped to stay a day or two longer, but I fear that my lord of Lincoln may have been followed here – or that somehow news of our meeting may have reached hostile ears. It may not be safe to remain. Go collect your things together so we can be ready to ride for Lowestoft tonight.'

'Then you will be coming with us to Flanders, my lord?'

'Of course.' His lordship's eyes darted back to me and he permitted himself a tight smile. 'I must see this through – for Richard – even if Earl John will not join us. Duchess Margaret expects me.'

That I had not been told. In fact, thinking back, I realized I had indeed been told very little. Not that Lord Francis would be here, certainly – just that the duchess's men would speak with the earl, and I should be ready to hand him the jewel and letter. But then, in truth, I was only a servant still – if at one of the grandest courts in all Christendom.

I bowed and, after a quick word to Alys and Elen, hurried to the chamber where I had laid my head that past night. It took little time to gather my few possessions, but even so, I had not finished when Lady Tyrell's serving man arrived to bid me make haste at once to the stableyard. Matters had, of a sudden, become urgent.

In the torchlit yard all was confusion. The horse I had ridden on our journey from the coast was standing patiently alongside several others, lit by the dimly glimmering flames, as stable boys and grooms milled about, readying harness and saddles. And among them – my heart almost stopped within me – was a pale grey stallion I had once known well.

I stood amazed, as though a ghost had emerged from the deep shadows of the night.

Lord Francis came up beside me.

'You recognize him, Matthew?'

'Aye, my lord. Storm. King Richard's favourite charger. Though I have not seen him since ...'

I stumbled to a halt, my mind reeling with memories.

'Since he carried me away from the battlefield, and then you to London?' said his lordship. How did he remain so calm? 'Your young friend Elen took him from Master Ashley's stables when the old merchant fled into exile – and had the presence of mind to bring him here. We shall take him across the sea to mount a true king again.'

'Aye, my lord, a true king.' My words trickled into my ears, but as though from a great distance. Lord Francis placed his hand on my shoulder and I felt the slightest squeeze.

'But tonight he will bear me again. Get yourself ready. We must leave as soon as we can. Lady Tyrell's men have warned of horsemen scouting the neighbourhood, though they do not know who they are or whom they serve,'

I shook away my recollections and rushed to my horse. As I affixed my bundle to the saddle, my Flemish companions and the Mallary brothers also hurried into the yard, each hefting his own baggage. They gave me good evening as they hastened to their mounts.

And then it struck me. I had not said my farewells to Alys and Elen.

As I hesitated, Lord Francis and the Burgundians swung themselves into their saddles, his lordship calling for me to follow their lead. But as the Mallarys stood checking their horses' bridles and girths, from the doorway of the stable building behind them erupted Alys herself, amongst a flurry of stable boys.

She was leading a grey pony, with Shadow gambolling round her heels and Elen, her arms outstretched, just behind. Alys was paying no attention to her friend, who was trying to hold her back. Instead, she was ordering the stable boys about. One slung and fastened a saddle across the pony's back even as it was walking forwards, another was tightening buckles on the bridle, a third hovering, holding a bundle and waiting to help Alys mount.

'My lady!' cried Lord Francis. 'What —?'

She swung round, her face sharp in the cold night air.

'I'm coming with you. You can't leave me here.'

'Indeed, I can, and I will,' he replied. 'You have no place in our company.'

'But, my lord —'

'Richard and Anne may have let you do as you pleased, but times have changed. You must remain here with Lady Tyrell.'

'But I beg you, my lord!' I had never seen Alys plead before. 'I have been here so long, alone. Waiting to find out what is to become of me. I cannot stay longer.'

'No, my lady.' His lordship's voice was firm. 'You must stay. Say your farewells to Matthew quickly. And if those unknown horsemen come to call, you will deny that we were ever here.'

Robert Mallary had taken hold of her pony's bridle and was now directing the stable boys to take the beast away, bowing to Alys almost as an afterthought.

She stood back to let them obey. Without a word, she accepted her bundle as it was handed back to her, all the fight knocked out of her.

I led my mount over.

'I'm glad to have this chance to say goodbye, Alys, and to you also, Elen.' I glanced past Alys to where the other girl stood quietly, the faintest of shadows upon her face. 'I feared for a moment Lord Francis would hurry us away before I did. I should not have been happy to have missed you.'

'Nor should I,' Alys said, but her attention was elsewhere. A mulish expression stole across her face as she stared after Lord Francis. He was taking his leave of Lady Tyrell on the front steps of the great house. The Mallary brothers were now mounted, and Robert was gesturing to me to make haste.

I took Alys's hand, but did not press it gallantly to my lips as Roger had done. Its slender fingers, though sheathed in kid-skin gloves, were cold as stone to my touch. I squeezed them lightly.

'I must go. I hope it will not be too long before we meet again.'

Her eyes slid back to me.

'I trust it will not too, Matt. I had hoped that … but no matter now. I must do as I am bid, whatever the outcome. Remember me to Edward and to Duchess Margaret. I hope I shall see them again soon. And you – take care and stay safe.'

A second later, I too was mounted and urging my horse to follow the other gentlemen out of the cobbled yard towards the lane away from Gipping Hall. Before we passed into the dark shadows of the tree-lined way, I glanced back over my shoulder.

The yard was empty now of stable lads and serving men. Only Alys and Elen remained in the glow of a single torch at the entrance. Elen had draped both her arms about her friend, but Alys stood upright within her embrace, as though too proud to shake it off. One hand grasping Shadow's collar, she was staring after us, no expression on her face.

I had no idea at that instant how long it would be before I met either of them again.

I had not reckoned, of course, on the approach of Lord Soulsby's men along the lane towards us only moments later, compelling us to hide in the field beyond the flint-studded chapel. Or on Alys's desperate flight away from them, or her pleas when she caught up with us, which finally forced Lord Francis to let her join our company on our night ride to the port of Lowestoft.

I had, for some reason, forgotten how Alys always, somehow, got her own way ...

5

Return to Lowestoft

The road into Lowestoft was as I remembered it, though I had not seen it before in the frosty light of a late autumn morning.

We all dismounted before the town began. Lord Francis was on edge. Something on our approach unsettled him. He pulled us and our mounts into a stand of trees for cover.

'I have spent a long time living on my wits this past year, and I've had to develop a nose for trouble,' he explained to the perplexed Burgundian gentlemen, as Alys and I looked on. 'Something isn't right here. Giles, you can blend easily into the background of such a town as this. Scout ahead and let us know what is amiss.'

Before long Giles was back, dodging from tree to hedge to tree as best he could. With him was a sailor from the ship in which we had sailed to England. Though he wore the same shirt and leggings as any sailor, English or foreign, I recognized his face from our days aboard.

'I met this lad on my way in, my lord,' Giles said, his voice hardly above a whisper. The sailor glanced over his shoulder as though from instinct, before bowing to his lordship. Giles continued, 'His captain had the good sense to set him to watch for us.'

Lord Francis nodded his head to the man in greeting.

'You have news for us?'

The sailor bowed again.

'Goedendag, meneer,' he said. 'My kapitein sent me as I speak a little English. There are men – in the town. Riders. They come in the night.'

Lord Francis cursed, then recovered himself, turning to apologize to Alys, as if only just remembering she was part of our company.

She was oblivious. Her eyes, staring at the sailor, suggested her ears also were fixed only on his report.

'Who are they?' his lordship asked. 'Do you know?'

The man shrugged, his hands spread wide.

'They are many. Ten, maybe more. They wear green, grey, a badge with a —' he searched for the right word in English and failed – though we all knew what it would be – 'a *raaf* – a big, black bird.'

'A raven,' translated Master van Ghendt, the senior of the emissaries. His English was impeccable, as I had discovered on our voyage.

'Soulsby's men,' breathed Giles Mallary.

'But they cannot have overtaken us, little brother,' said Robert. 'Even if they knew where we were headed. Surely. Not in the night.'

Lord Francis shook his head.

'Lord Soulsby has many men. Ten or more here. Half a dozen at Gipping, Matthew said. He has perhaps got wind of my movements – or of these gentlemen's arrival here,' he gestured to the Burgundians, 'and sent men to discover more. And a ship new in from the Low Countries – sitting in harbour here, neither loading nor unloading cargo, waiting – that will have piqued their curiosity.'

'But no, meneer,' spoke up Master van Ghendt. 'The ship and crew do not stand idle. Our mistress, the duchess, made certain that it would be a merchant ship. One well known in these parts. These past days it has been unloading Burgundian cloth and loading bales of wool to sell to weavers in Bruges after our return. It should attract no such attention.'

'Of course. I should have expected nothing less of your resourceful mistress.' Lord Francis bowed to the gentlemen. 'But Lord Soulsby's suspicions have been aroused none the less, if not by this particular ship.' He turned back to the sailor. 'Is the ship itself watched?'

'Nee, I think not. There are many ships in harbour

– from Sluis, Bruges, Friesland. They may not know which is ... which is ... *belangrijk*.'

'Which is important,' supplied Master van Ghendt once more. 'We may be able to slip past these men and aboard without too much trouble.'

'Especially if there is a distraction,' put in Robert Mallary.

'A distraction?' Lord Francis raised his eyebrows at him.

'Aye, my lord. Giles and I can draw Soulsby's men away while you gain the ship. If this lad can go ahead to make sure all is ready, once you are aboard you can set sail.'

'Without you?'

'I have no desire to see foreign parts. Good old England is enough for me and Giles.'

The younger man nodded, but with a small shrug. Did Robert truly speak for him too? But his brother paid no heed.

'And when you return at the head of the army of our new King Edward, we shall join you again – me and all my brothers.'

'Aye, then, old friend. But you must make certain of your own escape.'

The sailor was despatched back to arrange all that was necessary with his captain, while we laid plans for our escape. I kept watch for the agreed signal. From our hiding place I could just make out which of the ships clustered along the distant harbour wall was ours. Before too much time passed, a banner was hauled up the main mast: the flag of the port of Sluis from which I had set out only days before.

'The captain signals all is ready,' I reported to his lordship. And with few words more, our plans swung into action.

The two Mallary brothers shook hands with Lord Francis in farewell. Then, gathering together the reins of all the horses save Storm, they mounted their own beasts and, leading the others, rode off through the fields inland of the town.

Those of us who remained waited again.

Tension crackled among us and our breathing was shallow – barely pluming in the frigid air. Master van Ghendt passed the time counting his rosary. The click, click, click of the beads slipping along the cord drew a faint frown from Lord Francis, though he said nothing. But his gloved fist was tight as he gripped Storm's reins.

Alys shivered, and for the first time I perceived how little she wore – a light cloak only, enfolded now about her indoor gown. It must have been all she could snatch up in her rush to leave Gipping Hall.

On our ride there had been mercifully little wind to knife through us. The speed and effort had kept us – or me, at least – warm. Now I caught her eye, reaching up to unfasten the clasp of my thick, fur-lined cloak to offer it to her. But her hand grasped my own, before flying to her lips in a sign to silence me. Her quick ears had detected some sound on what breeze there was, and her finger pointed now to its source.

Some way inland from us, and towards the north of the town, on a little rise topped by scrubby willow trees a stream of dark grey smoke was rising into the pale sky. A flowering of red-gold flames. Then – the crack of a handgun. Another. Distant shouts of men. Two more shots.

Our signal to make a start.

Lord Francis waved me on ahead and with Alys's fingers now entwined in my own, I led the way into the town. As I had this past half hour or so, I prayed over and over to the Virgin and St Christopher that I would recall the streets of this place well enough to guide our steps.

Another volley of gunfire, more cries.

As we entered the main street, townsmen were emerging from their houses, rushing through the streets towards the upper end of town to discover what was afoot. Goodwives stood in doorways, wiping their hands on aprons, soothing children, craning to see, exchanging questions with neighbours.

One or two men and women glanced our way, but took no more notice, hurrying on, or chatting still. To a quick glance we were just a party of wayfarers, one horse between us, all decked in dusty travelling cloaks. These were clutched tight about the emissaries' fine Burgundian fashions and Alys had raised her hood to hide the brilliance of her light-red hair, as ever escaping her linen cap. Lord Francis had no trouble looking the part. I had seen his worn garb the moment he emerged the day before, though I now knew the tatters of his cloak helped conceal good armour beneath.

Everything in this town appeared very different in daylight and without sea fret swirling around us. But I recalled what Captain Hans, owner of the *Falcon* and our saviour last year, had told me then. All the alleys – or scores – to our right would lead to the harbour.

The bustle all about was growing. Shopkeepers dashing past clutching knives and cleavers, a blacksmith and apprentices running with hammers, fishermen stumping along carrying boat hooks. Evidently the town believed it was being attacked. Just what had been happening in England during my exile to make townspeople react this readily?

Did Alys see the question on my face as I paused, watching?

She tightened her grip on my hand.

'The townsfolk will take no chances with such disturbances in these troubled days. The brothers chose their tactics well. We must hope Lord Soulsby's men are as wary.'

'Hurry, Matthew,' Lord Francis called from our rear, and we pushed forward again, as more shots struck my ears above the chatter and shouts of the locals.

My eyes scoured the close-packed houses, inns and shops to the right for the first opening. And as I spied the black iron lantern hanging at its entrance, a low rumble grew ahead of us along the main street. The thudding of hooves on the frozen earth.

Lord Francis forced Storm beneath the overhanging upper storey of the nearest building, out of the way of any oncoming riders, ushering the rest of us after him. Alys seized Shadow's scruff and dragged her with us, into our huddle against the roughly plastered wall.

The drumming surged, hoofbeats now resounding about us in the narrow street. My heartbeat echoed them, thundering in my head as my chest tautened, and Alys's face paled in the shadows.

Yet we need not have worried. The horses were not approaching. Fifty, sixty yards ahead, a party of riders flashed right to left across the street, vanishing into a lane leading out of town, up the slope towards where the Mallarys had set their diversion. Too quick for me to count their number, or catch more than a burst of green–grey. The clamour of hooves soon dwindled and died to nothing.

More gunshots – one, two.

Lord Francis's face was grim.

'They must end it now and flee themselves. They've given us our chance. Come, Matthew – make sure it isn't wasted.'

I pointed at the welcoming entryway of the score – the first we had come to. A twinge of relief pricked at me: it was not the one I remembered so well from before. This one ran between two shops, their frontages and stacked wares deserted now, save for an infant standing crying in one doorway, holding up its tiny hands in a plea for comfort. Lord Francis plunged into the alley, drawing Storm, the emissaries and Alys with him. As I followed, I caught sight of a wide-eyed woman rushing forward to scoop the child away, back into the safety of the shop.

Once past the timber and plaster sides of the shops, this score led steeply down through brick and flint walls. Its floor was laid with small cobbles and Storm's hooves clattered as he trotted beside his lordship. Alys glanced back at me once, twice. Was she too haunted by memories of such a place? But I just waved her on after the others and followed at a run, peering over my shoulder now and then to check we were not pursued. But, indeed, who would chase us towards the harbour when the danger so clearly lay inland?

A sharp bend to the left revealed black timber jetties and steel-grey breakers framed by the end of the alleyway. The keen tang of salt air wafted into my nostrils. Where the score widened into the harbourside, the stone bulk of a tavern reared up on the corner, its swinging sign overhanging the alley's mouth. It creaked as it swung, and my eye was drawn upwards.

The sign was a boar's head – crudely painted.

And despite my hurry, for a moment time shuddered to a halt.

The paint on the sign was peeling in the harsh sea air. Blue shreds, like the bristles of the boar itself, were flaking away to reveal the white beast beneath.

The tavernkeeper had painted over His Grace King Richard's symbol, the white boar, with a newer colour.

It felt an age before I could compel my legs to move again. The others had already rounded the corner and as I scurried on to the wide harbourside, they were some yards ahead. Making for the fourth ship moored there – its banner with stout tower and red rampant lions fluttering on the topmast, above sails unfurled for its journey.

Alys, with Shadow bounding before her, was sprinting ahead of the others, her hood flopped down, her cap barely clinging to her streaming hair. Perhaps she was afraid she might still be left behind, even at this late stage. Storm's coat shone in the early sunlight glinting off the waves, his crest curving regally and his feet stepping high across the stone paving. The two Burgundians – neither young – were huffing with the speed of their flight, urged on by Lord Francis. He glanced back from time to time as he ran towards the gangplank, his ragged cloak fluttering in his wake.

I paused for a split second, wondering how Storm would approach the way on to the ship. Well trained he might be, but had he ever been aboard a swaying, heaving boat, tossed on the swell of the ocean? Would he even set hoof upon the narrow wooden plank that would lead him there?

As I hesitated, watching, movement at the corner of my eye wrenched my sight that way.

A figure loomed in the dark doorway of the tavern. A bulky figure, hastening out, adjusting the fastening of his grey and green doublet and calling to the stable lad holding a bay horse there on the harbourside. As I, at last, launched myself after my companions, his eye caught mine.

I knew him instantly. His was a face I would never forget.

Hugh Soulsby.

My shock was mirrored on his broad face. He had not forgotten me either.

His mouth opened, to shout, to call for aid perhaps.

But as I forced my feet on and sped towards the others, now boarding the ship, I heard no cries behind me, no stamping of boots in pursuit, felt no hot breath upon my neck, no hand grabbing at me to yank me down.

I made it to the gangplank just as Storm, his eyes covered by a blindfold, was stepping delicately off the far end and I tore across behind, making him dance upon his hooves at the rush of movement.

Yelling frantically, I dragged at nearby sailors, begging them to pull up the plank behind me. They did so, with wide, questioning eyes, not understanding the urgency.

As I gazed back to the harbourside, across their flustered activity, I spied Hugh's shadowy form standing still in the tavern doorway, the reins of his horse now in his hand.

And as I watched, my breath coming in great gulps in my fear, he calmly mounted and rode away into the dark, gaping mouth of the score, out of sight.

6

The Duchess

The approach to the palace in Mechelen was not grand. It had no splendid gatehouse, like that at Middleham Castle, and its severe white stone façade fronted on to the city street itself. But the ornate-liveried, heavily armed guards with their crossed halberds – alert to all comers – proclaimed it was the residence of a person of the highest importance.

And so she was. Margaret Plantagenet. Once princess of England and Duchess of Burgundy. Related by marriage to the emperor himself. Sister to two kings of England. And now aunt – in law – to a third.

I spat on the paving before the wide stone steps as the thought struck me. I was clearing my mouth of the dust of our long journey, of course. But at the same time, the notion that this gracious lady, family to my late master and to my new, should now be kin to the usurper through his wife, the Lady Elizabeth, was like a griping poison within me.

Her Grace was expecting us, a message having been sent on ahead of us by way of a swift rider from the port of Sluis. Lord Francis and Alys were escorted to their chambers to recover from the journey, while our two Burgundian companions were shown straight into the duchess's private chambers. And I made my own way to the small antechamber of my lord Edward's apartment, where my bed was set up, as usual when Edward was in residence. Edward was not in his rooms – summoned, I suspected, to his aunt to receive the emissaries and hear their report.

Relief trickled through me. I did not have to face him yet. For all Lord Francis's words, repeated on our crossing, I knew I would – must – take some blame for our failure to persuade the Earl of Lincoln. Could I have done more? I could not tell how. But Edward was unlikely to view it that way.

I poured water from a jug into the waiting basin to wash away the filth of the journey. For a few moments I stared down into the depths of the water. As the ripples settled, my reflection stared back up at me. Dark eyes blinked their tiredness beneath always-unruly brown hair. Then I plunged in both hands to splash my face and slick down that hair, before stripping off my travelling clothes and replacing them with clean livery laid out ready on my mattress.

This tiny room, amidst the labyrinthine passages of the palace – furnished only with bed, chest and wooden shutters at the windows to keep out the cold – had been my home off and on for many months now, since Edward had tossed and turned in the throes of his illness under the care and watch of the duchess's physicians. Under my watch too. I did not leave his side for all those weeks, save sometimes to eat with my friends, twice to bid them farewell, occasionally to wander the busy streets of this strange town to take the air. The duchess herself had spoken to me from time to time and insisted upon that. And on the first day that I had met her, I had been smitten by her likeness to my old master, her youngest brother.

Yet for all the time I had spent here, and all the kindness I had received from the mistress of the palace, it had never felt like a home – any more than did the other apartments where Edward had stayed while in Flanders. And now, after the brief taste I had had of England … now … would I ever find somewhere I would feel at home again?

I shook these thoughts away and stretched out on my mattress to rest until my summons should come. As it would – soon. I knew Edward was impatient to be moving on with his plans – whatever they now would be.

The knock on the door roused me from my doze and, with a quick run of my fingers through my still-damp hair, I followed the servant on the serpentine route to the duchess's reception chamber.

Alys and Lord Francis were there before me, now more fittingly attired for attendance at a court – Lord Francis sporting a doublet of deep red velvet trimmed with black fur, Alys in a gown of moss green, white fur at cuffs and neckline. Precious emeralds gleamed at her throat and a high headdress adorned her red-gold hair, caught up in and draped about with fine local lace. Her discomfort at the finery was scrawled across her face as she greeted me.

The lines of tension on Lord Francis's face had deepened in the time since I'd last seen him – or perhaps they had previously been disguised by layers of grime now cleansed away. If I dreaded the reception that awaited me, so too it seemed did he – as if we were two errant schoolboys awaiting our master's whip.

He did no more than nod at me before the entrance of the duchess was announced and we all bowed our deepest to the lady who swept in through the iron-edged double doors. Clad also in the richest silks, brocades and furs, her towering hennin added such height to her already tall frame that she resembled nothing so much as one of those splendid merchant galleys we had seen on our arrival at Sluis – in full sail and ready to set forth. Her ice-blue eyes and strong chin marked her out as the Plantagenet she was and always had been, no matter what family she had married into.

The figure who entered at her side could have been dwarfed by her, although he too had inherited his size from his father's family. But Edward would be put in the shade by no one – man or woman. Despite his illness, the past year had added to his stature – not just in height, and in muscle gained through resumed training, but also in his presence. Like his father, King Edward before him, he had an air of regality – as well as one of entitlement and privilege. To my eyes, he looked every inch the king he believed himself to be.

Yet it was, of course, his aunt who was first to speak.

'Viscount Lovell, we greet you well. Welcome to our court. And I am glad at last to offer you my thanks for your stalwart service to my lamented brother Richard, and your continued assistance to the Yorkist cause.'

Lord Francis bowed over her beringed hand to kiss it, though a spasm of pain flashed across his face as he did.

'I thank you also, Your Grace, for your welcome for a poor exile such as myself.'

'Not an exile for long, I hope, my lord. I trust you will soon make a triumphant return to the country you served so well as chamberlain.'

The duchess now turned her attention to Alys.

'And my lady Alys Langdown. I did not think to see you here again so soon.'

Two points of deep pink blossomed high on Alys's cheekbones, but she cast her eyes down demurely, as expected of her.

'Nor I indeed, Your Grace. But events beyond my control …'

She left the words hanging, but Duchess Margaret appeared content to let the matter rest – for the moment at least. Perhaps her emissaries' reports had been very detailed where Alys was concerned.

Now her sharp blue eyes were affixed on me.

'And Master Wansford. We had hoped to welcome your return under more favourable circumstances.'

Edward made a slight movement beside her and, not wanting to meet his gaze, I dropped to my knees before his aunt.

'Your Grace, I'm so sorry. I tried my best. But Lord Lincoln —'

I fell silent as I felt the soft touch of her hand on my head.

'Nay, Matthew, be not so distraught that your efforts did not meet with greater success. Come, stand up.

My gentlemen tell me they believe my nephew never meant to join us. That he only met with Lord Lovell and yourself at the urging of his mother.'

'Aye, madam,' agreed Lord Francis, as Ays helped pull me back to my feet. 'I believe that to be true. Though his sympathies lie with our cause, the earl has seen the failure of all efforts so far. He has no certainty that a further attempt will have more success.'

Edward thrust himself forward.

'My cousin does not believe that my countrymen will rally to my banner once I am made known to them?'

His voice was raw with disbelief.

'Edward,' Lord Francis hesitated, then corrected himself, 'Your Grace, on my travels through England this past year, when I have spoken of you to those I trust – good Yorkists, servants of your beloved father or uncle – they have expressed their disbelief that you still live. Those rumours put about during the rebellion against your uncle – that you and your brother had perished in the Tower, or in shipwreck as you were spirited abroad – they took strong root. We saw the fruit of that when your uncle took on Tudor in battle. Too many chose not to fight that day.'

'As well they might,' retorted Edward. 'Perhaps he did not have us killed or sent aboard ship to our death, but I can never forget or forgive his actions that stole my crown.'

'Soft, Edward,' said the duchess, placing a hand on his shoulder. 'That is in the past now. My brother did what he believed right at the time. You forget the problems that your father left behind at his early death. He would not have intended what occurred – nor did our brother Richard. But the situation was as it was – and now we must deal with the circumstances as they are.'

Edward's mouth clamped shut. King he might be, but perhaps here, now, he knew he was no more than a boy, a guest in a foreign land. And I knew he had heard all this before.

Lord Francis returned to his point.

'When I meet with such men, it helps to show them letters from you and from Her Grace, but still they doubt. They hear one thing from me, another from their neighbour, something else put out by the usurper. What should they believe in these times? Tudor is gradually gaining control of the country. He entices one lord to his side, he threatens another, the next knows not which way to turn, but sees another begin to prosper at Tudor's hand.'

He sighed, weariness and frustration battling upon his face.

'Had we perhaps been able to move a year ago, even earlier this year, while Tudor's grip and his government were more uncertain. When there was still unrest – cities, whole regions simmering with resentment, ready to rise against Tudor as Worcester, Nottingham, York did – we might have had more chance.'

'But I could not then, Lord Lovell. My life was still in peril.' Edward forced his words out as though through clenched teeth.

'I know, Your Grace – it was not possible. But had it been, many men would not have thought twice about flocking to you. Lord Lincoln among them, I'm sure, for all his father's apparent loyalty now to the usurper. Lord Surrey too – maybe Northumberland even. Tudor imprisoned both because he doubted them. That might well have helped to ensure their allegiance to you.'

'Again, Lord Lovell, it is now we must think of.' The duchess's words drew a bow of the head in agreement from his lordship. 'If Lincoln will not join us, what is your counsel?'

'Perhaps we should look to Ireland,' he replied. 'The FitzGeralds were ever loyal to both your brothers. Earl Gerald of Kildare has kept his appointment as Lord Deputy under Tudor, but only because the usurper can find no other to trust in the job – and he fears what Kildare will do if he loses his position. And perhaps —' he hesitated, glancing at Edward, 'perhaps an approach could be made to Your Grace's mother, the dowager queen.'

'She will support me, of course,' insisted Edward, 'in any way she can.'

'But,' Lord Francis spoke slowly, as though choosing his words with utmost care, 'circumstances, as we have said, have changed, Your Grace. Now your sister … now your sister Elizabeth is not only married to Tudor, but mother of his child – and a son at that – it may be that your lady mother – that she —'

'That my mother's allegiances may also have changed?' Bitterness stained Edward's words. I flinched at the sound. 'Why not say it? She betrayed me once before – choosing to flee to sanctuary with my sisters after my father's death, rather than stay to take charge of Richard and me. She should have protected me better from what my uncle did.'

'She could not have gone against Parliament, Edward.' The duchess's voice was calm and even. 'It was Parliament that put you and your brother aside, not Richard.'

'Aye,' agreed Lord Francis. 'And I was with your uncle during those days and weeks after Bishop Stillington came forward – when Stillington presented his evidence of your parents' unlawful marriage to the Royal Council. Richard did not find it easy to make those decisions – to investigate further, to have evidence of his brother's misdeeds reported publicly to Parliament, to accept the Lords and Commons' decision to disinherit you. Or to take on the burden of the crown.'

'Yet he did make those decisions,' fired back Edward. 'And at least he had a choice. I did not.'

'Edward,' his aunt said, her tone sharp. 'You forget yourself.'

Edward's eyes flicked from her, to me, then to Alys, and his colour rose.

'My mother will support me, I'm sure of it.'

And he pivoted on his heel and strode towards the doors – opened hurriedly by the servants to let him through, then closed with a soft click behind his retreating back.

The atmosphere in the chamber was charged with discomfort, as though with static before a storm.

Alys's eyes sidled towards me, her brows raised in a query. She, of course, had not seen Edward since he had recovered from his wound, and perhaps my report to her on our journey had been less detailed that that of Her Grace's ambassadors. But it was not our place to speak now.

After an uneasy moment, the duchess broke the silence.

'I'm sorry, Lord Lovell. You must forgive him. He is a boy still, for all his manly appearance, and we must admit he has had great burdens of his own to bear these past years.'

Lord Francis bent his head to her again.

'His wound and illness brought him low,' she continued, 'and he has succumbed also to melancholy in the months since his bodily recovery. Young Richard tells me their physician attended him for it often in the Tower after his father died and his mother …'

She checked herself.

'I have no love for Elizabeth Woodville, as you may be aware, but it was my brother Edward's choice to be led by her in many things. And after he died, I supported my brother Richard in doing what he thought best to deal with the problems that were caused. But now we have different problems to deal with, and I shall do what I think best. If that involves negotiating with Elizabeth for the good of England and my family, so be it.' Her manner softened a little. 'Though it will be difficult for her. To choose between two children —'

'Three children,' Lord Francis reminded her. 'If she chooses Elizabeth and the grandchild over Edward, she also abandons young Richard.'

'True. It is not a choice I would wish on anyone, even my dearest enemy.'

For an instant, the duchess's blue eyes seemed directed inward, and I recalled that she had never had children herself. What had been her feelings over the years when news kept coming from England of yet another child born to her brother's wife? Yet almost at once her imperious tone returned.

'But we must put it to her if we can. Marriages can be annulled. Princess Elizabeth can start anew if her brother wins his throne. Who would turn down the chance to marry the sister of the King of England, no matter who her first husband?'

Alys raised a hand to brush some errant lace away from her face and the movement caught the duchess's attention.

'Meanwhile, my lord, we have much to discuss, and it does not need the presence of these young people. Perhaps we should retire to my private chamber and allow them to go about their own business.' She fixed us both with her glacial gaze. 'Mayhap they can reacquaint themselves with my nephew. It would perhaps do them all much good.'

With a courteous nod to Alys and me, she swept from the chamber, drawing Lord Francis and the servants in her stately wake. And, at long last, I was left alone with Alys.

We were both silent for a moment, then she looked at me, a strange, shy smile upon her lips.

'Was that a command from Her Grace do you think, Matt?' she asked.

'Aye, I believe so.'

And as one we made our way from the chamber too.

I was disappointed, of course. I would have liked to speak with her privately. It was the first time I had been alone with her for so many months.

But perhaps there was the difficulty. Once again our paths had diverged and then recrossed, and we were older again, and had had different experiences and seen different things. We had spoken much when we had been here before, when we could be spared during Edward's illness and could escape any chaperone – talking of all we had lived through during our two years apart, of what we had not said in our many letters, and of the terrors and fears of our last weeks, days, hours in England. But now we had been apart once more ... it was almost as though we had to begin our friendship again.

7

Edward

Edward himself called to us to enter when we knocked at the door to his chamber. It appeared he had dismissed his attendants – all of them – and he lay now upon his finely carved tester bed, propped up by feather bolsters, his swordbelt discarded on the floor and a small leather-bound book unopened in his hand. Late afternoon sunlight filtered through the costly glass in the window, touching silver thread on the tapestried walls to flame, and in the small fireplace, a cheering fire danced against the chill.

Alys and I advanced into the room and bowed to him.

'Yes?'

The single word and the expression on his face told that the fire had not done its job – cheer was far from his mind.

Alys was silent, watching him, but the pointed toe of her embroidered slipper nudged my leather boot.

As ever at her command, I started forward.

'Your Grace, the Duchess Margaret sent us to enquire after you.'

Edward's eyes rolled heavenwards, then closed with a heavy tiredness. It was a moment before they opened again and he stared directly at me.

'Matthew, before you went away you had begun to call me Edward again, as in days past. Perhaps one day I may truly be king. But for now … I know I owe you my life, you and Alys. For now, let me be just plain Edward to you both again. And,' he cast his gaze about, around, behind us, 'and Roger? Is he not here? I didn't see him in the receiving chamber. I thought he was to be with you? I have not seen him since … since my illness. I remember him here then – I think.'

Alys stepped towards him in her turn.

'Roger remained in England, Edward. With … on his father's instructions.'

Her untruth about his reason for staying startled me. Yet it was perhaps only a white lie – one to save a painful reminder of Earl John's decision.

Her hesitation passed Edward by.

'I'm sorry for that. He was a welcome distraction. And your hound, Alys? Where is she? Matthew told me what happened to Murrey, but I had hoped to see Shadow again.'

'She's in my chamber. It would not have done to have her with me when we were received by your aunt. But I could fetch her now if you wish?'

And at a word from him, her departure to the far side of the palace led to the moment I had dreaded.

Edward watched me steadily a short while, before motioning me to sit on a nearby stool. He himself continued to recline upon the bed.

'So, I gather your embassy to my cousin did not go well.

'No, it didn't.'

Perhaps my answer should have been less abrupt, maybe more contrite. But what more did he want me to say? He had listened to his aunt's emissaries, been with us when the matter was discussed by the duchess and Lord Francis. What else could I tell him?

If he noticed my shortness, he did not heed it.

'Did you give him my letter?'

'Of course. And Lord Lovell read it after and agreed it was a good letter. But he reckoned nothing could have changed the earl's mind.'

'Did you show him my jewel?'

Edward's eyes had taken on a shade of wintry blue, glittering like flint in the cool daylight. And I realized my tardiness. It was not wise to make such mistakes around him.

I thrust my hand into the depths of my pouch and

withdrew the heavy blue velvet bag, its gilt fastening glimmering in the firelight.

I handed it to him.

'Yes, Edward, and he knew of it, and recognized it was from you. But it did not sway him – except perhaps to accept you are who you say you are. Who we said you are.'

He grunted, loosened the cord, tipping the shining gold chain out upon his hand, then stowed the bag and its contents among his bolsters.

'You seem to have done your duty.'

'Of course, Your — Edward.'

He paused, opening, then closing the book in his hand.

'But did Lovell? After all, he also was my uncle Richard's man. And I see he still wears my uncle's boar badge upon his chest to show his loyalty – as you do, despite my displeasure.'

I made no answer. All this ground had been well trodden over recent months. I saw no reason to journey across it again.

But Edward – Edward always did.

'He was there, you know. Lord Lovell. Throughout those weeks. When my uncle stole my throne. Though I have not met him since ... until today. Yet my aunt insists that I must trust him.'

'I'm sure she has good reason.' I felt he expected me to say something at least. 'She trusted King Richard, and Lord Francis was his especial friend. King Richard trusted him in all things.'

But Edward's mind was running on one path only.

'Is that reason for me to? He tried to persuade me that my uncle was my friend when we were in London. Was that true? And when —' He swallowed. 'When the slanders about my parents began, he came with my uncle to tell me what was happening. He told me later that my uncle believed he owed it to me.'

Edward's face was pinched, his eyes narrowed,

incredulous at the memory. But I could believe it. It sounded just like the man I had known.

'They came together that day, to our chambers in the Tower. When the knock came at the door and the servant announced the Lord Protector, I was filled with dread. I knew something was afoot. There had been whispers. Servants, even the lowliest maids, cast glances askance at me. But no one told me anything.'

He was no longer looking at me, his whole focus now directed inward, towards that day more than three years before.

'At first my uncle had visited me frequently, both at the Lord Bishop's palace, then when I moved to the Tower to await my coronation. Though he and the Royal Council had delayed the coronation by then, of course. To make certain, he said, that it was done properly, not rushed. That all should be full of pomp and magnificence, as it always had been – all the nobles and great men of the realm present, all the ambassadors from abroad. He told me that himself.'

He paused, remembering still.

'He spoke to me always as he had at Stony Stratford – as though I were a real king, no longer a child, though I was but twelve years old. An adult to whom he spoke as a friend. Though one he also served, as he had my father. But I did not want to talk to him – wanted only my mother – or my uncle Rivers, my brother Grey.'

The men who were later tried and executed, I recalled, for their treasonous attempted ambushes on the road to London. But I said nothing. As ever, Edward was raking over only the still-white-hot coals of his personal betrayals.

'But my mother did not come. Nor my brother Dorset. They preferred to stay in sanctuary rather than face what was to come. But they knew, didn't they? They knew the guilty secret. They knew what that would mean for me and Richard.'

The guilty secret. That his mother had married his

father when his father's first – secret – wife still lived. That he and young Richard were not true sons of the king, born safe in wedlock, but illegitimate and unable to inherit the crown.

'So, it fell to my uncle Gloucester to tell me – he and his henchman, Lovell. Barely family, for all he was my father's brother. I hardly knew him.'

I remembered from my days with them at Northampton – their strained conversations, the attempts by Duke Richard to befriend the young Edward. The boy's bewilderment at the loss of his uncle Rivers, at the news of his mother's flight to sanctuary. His suspicion of those who now had care of him. What had Rivers and the old queen, Edward's mother, told him of his uncle Richard before then that so worried him?

'It was a warm evening when they came ...'

As many had been that early summer, I remembered ...

People had gathered on street corners in the late sunshine after the day's work was finished, and talked and chewed over the latest news. As rumours and tales swilled through the thoroughfares like the rancid sewage flushing through the gutters. About the late king, why the queen had fled to sanctuary, what was whispered about their marriage. About what the Duke of Clarence might have known, why he was executed, the reason Lord Hastings had lost his head ...

'We had been in the pleasure gardens much of the day, Richard and I. Yet the pages had not wished to play at our games with us, servants glanced to one side so as not to catch our eyes, withdrew from us as we passed back to our chambers. We asked them questions. They claimed to know nothing – or that they had been sworn to silence.'

He paused a moment, and when he spoke again, his voice was spiked with resentment.

'And then came that knock on the door.'

He had told me the story of this meeting before, but every time, I listened. It seemed to help Edward when someone listened to him. And each time I did, my master stood before me again. It was as though I saw him and heard him speak once more.

'The Lord Protector, Your Grace.'

The servant announcing the new arrivals had bowed low and withdrawn, back into the corridor, though leaving the door ajar. Duke Richard had motioned to Lord Francis to close it securely against any listeners as he walked towards his nephew. He was wearing dark mourning clothes, though Edward noticed a change to a deep purple hue.

'Your Grace.' The duke had bowed his head. 'Edward. I beg leave to speak with you on an important matter. A personal one, and also, I'm afraid, a matter of state.'

Edward had straightened up, standing tall before his uncle. Though only a boy of twelve, his inheritance of his father's height meant their eyes were almost level. But his voice quavered as he replied.

'And is it for my brother Richard to stay and listen too?'

Something, a shadow perhaps, had flitted across Duke Richard's face. He glanced at the younger boy, sitting in the shafts of evening sunlight barring the window seat, casting dice alone. The boy's blue eyes were wide beneath his crop of fair hair as he turned, hearing his name.

'Richard is but young yet,' the duke had said softly. 'It may be best that he should leave us. And perhaps that you should be seated. I have much to tell you.'

'But I did not sit,' said Edward. 'As Richard departed to our sleeping chamber, I still stood – and forced my uncle and his man to stand also. A duke cannot sit when his king remains standing. And at that time, I was still his king – or so I believed.'

A smile without humour curled his lips.

'And so he told me. All of it – all that was known, at least, or thought to be known. About my parents' marriage – or what it really was. Gently as he thought it – though it tore at me inside like a hawk tears at the flesh of its prey. And then our positions were reversed. He told me he was to be king in my stead.'

But still they had stood. Until Duke Richard began to pace about the room.

'I wish it were not so, Edward,' he had said, as he reached the now empty window and cast an unseeing glance outside. 'I wish your father had not made these mistakes. I wish all this had not been told to me by Bishop Stillington. But the council had to know, had to act upon it, check the truth of the matter. And they have done. And it seems that the bishop spoke the truth. That he did indeed conduct the marriage of your father to the lady Eleanor – before your father ever met your mother.'

Did Edward rant, or rage, or weep hot tears at hearing these words? He did not say.

'Then I am not to be king any longer?'

The duke had been silent, standing now before the great stone-carved fireplace, his hands upon the mantel, staring down into the long-empty grate.

'What shall happen to me? And my brother? My sisters – Elizabeth, Cecily ... Shall we be cast upon the streets to beg our bread?'

His uncle had swung round to face him, with a laugh – though the strain within it had been clear.

'Be not so dramatic, Edward! You are still the sons of a king, and your sisters his daughters. Even if you may not rule after him, you shall still live as befits your station.'

'And how is that? Perhaps it is not a life I would wish for. I was brought up to be king, trained to rule since I was a small child. What else is there for me?'

His uncle had watched him for a moment, one emotion following another across his face. Lord Francis had stepped forward, as though he would speak instead, but Duke Richard raised his hand to halt him.

'Edward, it is a hard reversal for you to stomach,

but you must accept it like a man. Like the king you would have been. The way you have been taught to behave. You and your brother will live as a nobleman's sons – in training to serve as we all do, until you are of age. Your sisters ... when your mother leaves sanctuary with them, I will ensure they are well provided for, and that they are married to good men.'

It was Edward's turn to laugh without mirth – to me, now, though his eyes were still directed to the past.

'To "good men". Yet now my sister Elizabeth is wife to ... That was another of his promises he didn't keep.'

'But —' I began. I wanted to say, 'But he didn't have time to. He was doing his best – even to the last,' remembering those days more than a year before when I heard of King Richard's marriage plans for his niece – and for himself. But knowing better than to defend my old master to my new, I ceased my protest.

Edward didn't heed my interruption.

'I did not answer him then, of course. I don't think he liked that.'

'My wife, your aunt, urged me not to do this,' the duke had continued, 'not to come and tell you myself. I see now that perhaps she was right. But who else could? Your mother ...' He hesitated, trying to choose the right words to speak to this sullen boy before him. 'Your mother is not available, nor your brother Dorset. I am your closest other relative – though you scarcely know me. I wish that were different. That we had known each other better, so that now —'

Edward had turned away, presenting his back to his uncle. His uncle who would now be king.

Duke Richard had continued to speak, his voice even.

'But perhaps now we can change that. I hope you will remain at court, you and your brother – for some time at least before you go elsewhere and continue your training.'

Edward did not reply.

The silence had lengthened.

Lord Francis had placed a hand on his friend's arm.

'We can do no more here, Richard. Let us leave him time to think on what you have said.'

The duke – now king – had been silent a few moments, gazing at the boy's rich velvet-clad back, its shoulders hunched against the pity in those clear blue eyes, under their frown-furrowed brow.

'I will do what I can, Edward, to make this change as easy as I can for you – and your brother. Do you wish me to tell him – or shall I send some lady to speak with him?'

He had left the suggestion hanging. The boy's unresponsive back repelled it without moving.

The duke's fingers twisted his ruby ring in his familiar gesture. The quietest of sighs.

'You are still my nephews, Edward, still of royal blood. Your life – and that of your family – is tied to the court. You are still part of the royal family. Not everything need change.'

'Perhaps he really believed that, wanted it even. But the more I heard, the more I thought ...' Edward's voice altered now, his face contorting with the words. 'When Lady Stanley came ... when she told us her son, Henry Tudor, would come back, fight my uncle Richard, overturn the decision of Parliament, place me on the throne ... And then that night in July, when my uncle had been crowned, was on his progress round the country ... when my lord of Buckingham sent word to us ... when her men came for us, with swords, and they fought, and killed our servants who opposed them ... and then were captured and taken away ... I didn't know who to believe, who to trust ...'

He swung his legs down from the bed and himself began to stride around his chamber, clutching the small book still in his hand.

'It all changed then. The Duke of Norfolk it was who came to see us this time. Told us we must move our apartments, deeper within the Tower. He redoubled our guards, while my uncle decided what to do next. For our own safety, he said, to stop any more attempts at kidnap. We would not be at court when my uncle returned – not even if we chose to now. It might not be safe. That's what he said – told us my uncle had said that. But it was just an excuse – to ship us off to who-knew-where – away from my mother, her supporters, who might have helped us.'

He heaved a huge sigh, frustrated, angry still.

'Afterwards, I fell into such a melancholy as never before. And it was all my uncle's doing. First he stole my throne, then he destroyed our lives. He said we were still his nephews – but would a true uncle have done what he did?'

He whirled now towards me, challenge in his eyes, his words.

This time, for the first time in all those months, I rose to it, as my old master faded into the shadows. I found my voice at last.

'If he felt it to be right.'

Surprise widened his eyes.

'And do you? Think it was right?'

'Perhaps. He was a good man.' Of that I had always been sure. 'I have no doubt he believed it was for the best.'

'Do you think he truly believed I was a ... Was my parents' marriage really illegal?'

Now I was silent. His question was unfair. How could I know that? And I could not speak against his parents.

Yet he twisted my silence against me – and against King Richard.

'See! You were – still are – his man. As Lovell is. And even you cannot defend him!'

'But Edward, once the council knew of your father's first marriage ... once Parliament ...'

I cast my memory back to those tumultuous, confused, frightening days in London, and before, on the road there. To what I had heard, been witness to. To the shadowed eyes and tired face of the man I had seen later, when he had just become king. And to his words on that last morning …

'The situation could not then be changed. And it didn't rest easy on your uncle. Perhaps even he wondered if he had been right. But he did what he thought right at the time. He was worried about the country, that civil war would flare again. Worried even …' a long-ago evening in Northampton returned to me, 'even, perhaps, about his wife and son – that they too might be in danger.'

'Yet they died anyway.' Edward's words scythed through my memories.

'Edward!'

My shock at his words must have been plain to him. A spasm twitched across his face, and he flung himself into a chair, dropping his book upon the nearby table and grasping instead a goblet that stood there waiting. He drank deeply and placed it back.

'I'm sorry, Matthew,' he said, his gaze cast down, his passion subsided. 'I know my aunt was a good woman. Even my mother said that. And … and my cousin Ed … But I knew nothing of him.'

In the quiet that followed, my thoughts drifted back to my old friend. Little Ed – so lively, so impetuous, so keen to grow up and serve his king. But also so delicate, as Roger once called him.

The fire in the grate had died back to glowing embers and I shivered.

A rap on the door broke the moment. It opened to reveal Alys, with Shadow slinking into the room at her skirts. The dog's ears pricked as though hearing the echoes of our talk, and Alys halted, her sharp eyes flicking to me in a question.

I shook my head in a tiny movement, my lips in a tight smile as I stood and drew away from them both. At a side table, I poured more wine, while Alys crossed the room towards the boy still slumped in his seat. Shadow trotted before her, thrusting her muzzle into his hands, loose upon his lap, and in a sudden movement, Edward buried his face in the rough white fur of her head.

A gentle thud, then hiss rose from the fire as the remains of a log fell and sparks flew.

Making her way behind Edward's chair, Alys placed her pale hand upon his shoulder, hunched as it was over her uncomplaining hound. His hand stole up to hers, took it, squeezed it once, then let go as he pushed himself up from his seat and strode towards the window. He stood there, staring out on to the street for some minutes. The shouts of street sellers hawking their wares wafted up to us from below.

I busied myself passing a cup of wine to Alys, then stirring the fire to enliven its embers. Alys seated herself nearby, sipping at her drink, watching Edward, while Shadow curled up to sleep at her feet. I envied the hound. That she could settle like that in the presence of a king. I took up my own position, behind Aly's chair, waiting.

The flames had flared back into life and again cast fleeting shadows about the chamber before Edward turned towards us. He took up his goblet again, but did not return to his seat, standing instead in front of the fireplace as though to warm himself. His face was brooding as he finally broke the silence.

'Perhaps my uncle was right after all. Perhaps I am not fated to be king.'

Alys threw a glance up at me, before she said, 'Not fated? Why do you say that?'

'My cousin Lincoln is not willing to fight for me. Maybe others in England will view it the same way.'

'He is only one man,' she replied, 'and he has his own reasons. Valid they may seem to him. But many others don't think like he does. They will flock to join you. Always better for them a Plantagenet – son of a great king, however —' she hesitated, 'whatever doubt there may have been – better a son of Edward the Fourth than a usurping tyrant.'

'Is he a tyrant?'

'He has all the makings of one. Lady Tyrell told me he has brutally crushed several rebellions, even dragging men from sanctuary to execute them. And when Lord Francis tried to stir revolt in York last spring, it is said men were offered pardons, but then hanged without trial after they gave themselves up to his men.'

Quiet reigned again for a time.

I took my seat on the stool, nursing my own winecup. Though I sipped from it from time to time, I didn't wish to dull my senses. It had been a long, tiring day, yet now this meeting had an air of importance for our futures.

When Edward spoke once more, his tone hadn't changed. It was as though Alys's arrival had shifted his thoughts on to a different path.

'And I am only sixteen – a boy still.'

Alys put down her goblet and leaned forward in her chair.

'Your father was only eighteen when he fought the battle at Towton and claimed his kingdom. Only two years older.'

'But he had campaigned alongside his father before that.'

'Sadly, though, your grandfather had died months before your father's victory.'

'A victory won with the support of his cousin.'

'The Earl of Warwick? True. But it may be that you will have the support of your cousin too. Lord Lincoln may yet change his mind. We had to flee Gipping before he had the chance. And you do have Lord Francis and your aunt Margaret – perhaps even Duke Maximilian will back you. Also you have the goodwill of many people in England.'

In the silence that followed, shadows crept across

the rich tapestries, the light now draining from the late afternoon sky. Closing the shutters, I thrust a taper into the fire to light the candles in sconces dotted about the room. Edward threw himself back into his chair by the fireplace and sat staring into the flames as though they could help him make up his mind. Yet Alys was in no mood to leave him in peace until he did.

'Of course, no one will blame you if you decide not to return to England. It must be your choice.'

'They will say I'm a coward if I do not go – not a true Plantagenet.'

'Who will?' Alys shot back. 'Not I!'

I said, 'You once told me your aunt said you could stay here as long as you wished.'

Edward's eyes were bleak, the flames reflected in their depths, as he looked first at Alys, then across to me. But I had to speak, had to continue.

'You could wait. You don't have to decide at once.'

'What? Wait until Tudor has strengthened his rule further? Had more sons? Till men have forgotten that I ever existed?'

'They will never do that.' Alys's voice was calm, encouraging. But did I detect some uncertainty? Perhaps Edward did too.

'You think so? Lord Lovell said I have already delayed too long – though I had no choice in the matter. It is now three years – more – since the people of London cheered me as their new king. Time has passed. They have welcomed – endured – two more kings since then, and few people have seen me in the meantime. They would not know me now.'

'They will if they are told you have returned.'

'Really?'

'Other cities too. I'm sure of it. Your father was well loved by the people, your grandfather too. And you may not choose to believe it, but so also was your uncle Richard. While I was at Lady Tyrell's, we had word that the council of York,' her glance flicked to me, 'risked Tudor's anger by lamenting your uncle's death and saying he had been murdered "to the great heaviness of the city". You are their kin, now their legitimate heir. The people will support you, will fight to win your crown for you – so long as we can persuade them you are who you say you are.'

'But perhaps there may lie the problem.' Some other light now flickered in Edward's eyes. 'Lord Francis said many now believe me dead – that my uncle or my lord of Buckingham disposed of me and my brother. Can we convince all – across that wide country – that we still live?'

8

The Book of Deeds of Arms and Chivalry

Over the coming days many councils took place at the palace – the duchess with her advisers, the emissaries I'd travelled with, Lord Francis, with representatives of her son-in-law, Duke Maximilian, who would one day be emperor after his father. Sometimes with Edward himself, although often not.

He had told his aunt of his decision on that first evening after speaking with Alys and me in his chamber – his decision to reclaim his throne from Tudor. Her counsel had been to wait a while, to consider some more, to make certain his mind was made up. But I think perhaps they both knew that a Plantagenet, once decided upon a course of action – however impetuous that choice might seem – was not to be shaken from that path.

No word had come from the Earl of Lincoln, and before long none was expected. Lord Francis asked to speak privately with Edward on the day after our arrival and, though his reception at first was frosty, as time passed they met more often and for longer. And his lordship was not the only one to have that privilege.

A week or so later, Alys sought me out in Duchess Margaret's pleasure gardens during a break from my duties.

'Reading? As always.'

Her voice startled me out of my reverie. I glanced up to where she stood over me, clutching a new brown-furred mantle close. A chill breeze was stealing through the bare branches of the ornamental trees and bushes, and her breath plumed in the air.

I leapt to my feet, snapping shut my book.

'Don't be daft, Matt. You needn't stand up for me.' She sat down on the wooden bench, taking the leather volume from my half-frozen hands. 'You have time to read, despite your duties for Edward? Is it poetry?'

As I lowered myself again to sit beside her, her lithe fingers leafed through the book to its richly decorated title page, then paused.

'Christine de Pizan? *The Book of Deeds of Arms and Chivalry.*' She raised her eyes to mine. 'Battle strategy? Not your usual taste.'

'The duchess still allows me to borrow from the palace library. But I read all the poetry while you were in England. It was only ten shelves' worth after all – barely even a week's reading, let alone a year's.'

My lame attempt at a joke, even with an accompanying smile, didn't fool her.

'Oh, Matt – were you so very lonely? In your letters – those that reached me anyway – you always seemed so cheerful.'

'No, not at all,' I protested. 'Everyone here is very friendly, I had new duties to learn, another language to perfect, Edward to – well, to assist in whatever way he required. And I've been continuing my training with the duchess's weapons master whenever we are here at the palace. I've scarcely had time to think, let alone be lonely.'

A serious expression settled on her face.

'Perhaps that would be a blessing. No time to think, to brood.'

I had no need to ask her what she meant, after this past year or two. We were silent together for a while before she spoke again.

'But at least now things are happening – plans being made that may change things for the better. Edward tells me a date has been set for him to sail for Dublin.'

'For Dublin? In Ireland? So it has been arranged?'

A pang struck me inside, but I batted it away. Whatever petty jealousy I might feel – that I wasn't involved in any planning, that Edward now confided more in Alys than in me – was unimportant compared with what was afoot.

'So Edward says. The duchess has not yet had any message from Lord Kildare, of course – there hasn't been enough time. But his gentleman here in Mechelen has assured her of his master's goodwill and willingness.' She hesitated. 'And there has been no word yet from Dame Grey.'

That would hurt Edward – not to have heard from his mother. London, after all, was so much closer than Ireland. Even though there might be difficulties in communicating with a lady at court under the Tudor usurper's nose, ways could be found. But I said nothing about that.

'So Edward is still determined to go?

'It seems so.' Her eyes flicked up at me, then down at the book in her hand. 'And you? You appear to be making preparations.'

The blood flooded to my cheeks.

'I must go where my master directs.'

'Is that how you see him?'

'Of course. The king ... King Richard told me I must scrvc him wcll.'

But had he? I told everyone this – had done since those dark, evil days after my first master's death, during our escape from England, through the fraught journey from the small port in Friesland towards the duchess's court at Mechelen. When we had to prove many times who we were and why we sought sanctuary with that great lady.

But today, as so often, I questioned myself. And Alys, as perceptive as ever, was staring at me. Did she sense my doubt? Though I had seen less of her than I would have liked since our arrival in Flanders, it had not taken long to fall back into our old, close ways.

'But surely you did all that King Richard could have asked of you – bringing Edward here, saving him on the way. You aren't bound to him for life.'

'Maybe not. But I feel it's what I must do for now. And if Edward expects me to ...'

'It's a long, dangerous journey over the sea to

Ireland. Especially in winter.'

I felt her shiver, despite the thick cloak that hung between us.

'I trust in God to keep us safe,' I said. Was my voice as steadfast as I hoped? 'And the skill of our brave Flemish sailors.'

Alys laughed. 'Let us hope that will do the trick. They both provided us good service at Lowestoft.'

Her words flung me back to the morning of our most recent escape from that town – and the familiar figure I had run into there. For some reason – I knew not why – I had mentioned the encounter to no one. My hurry and fear I had pinned on a sighting of Lord Soulsby's men approaching the harbour – not on one single such person. What prompted me to reveal it now to Alys I could not tell.

'Hugh was there that morning.'

'What?'

'Hugh – Hugh Soulsby. He was coming out of a tavern on the quayside when I passed it.'

'Hugh? But ... you didn't mention that. Oh, Matt, you must have been ...' She stopped, but shock was scrawled across her face, telling me what she thought.

'Terrified? Yes.' Why deny it? 'And angry.'

'Angry?'

'At what he did. At what I didn't do.'

We had talked about it all, at length, more than a year ago, but still I was haunted. Still I couldn't let go of what had happened, of that part of my past.

'That you didn't kill him? But truly you did the right thing, Matt.'

'Did I?' I had never been sure. And now, these past days ...

'Yes.' Alys, as always, was firm – as a rock. Her face too was stony. 'Did he recognize you?'

'Of course. I don't think anyone would ever forget the face of someone who tried to kill them – and failed.'

I forced a laugh. But I couldn't make light of it, no

matter how hard I might try – and the sound was eerie, unreal.

Alys brushed it aside.

'What did he do? I didn't see anyone on the harbourside when we set sail.'

That I could not explain, though I had turned it over and over in my mind so often since.

'Nothing. I don't know why. When I looked back, I expected to see him chasing after me, or at least hear him hollering for the other men. But he just mounted his horse and rode off back up the score.'

Alys's brow was furrowed, perplexed – as my own must have been at the time.

'But if he recognized you ... He knew who was with you last time he saw you in Lowestoft. Did he see us? Lord Francis?'

I thrust my memory back to that mad dash across the quay. To the huffing Burgundians, to Alys's red-gold hair streaming in the pale sunlight, to his lordship in his tatters.

'I'm not sure. You may all have been aboard by then. Storm was just stepping off the gangplank when I ran up.'

'Perhaps not then.' She was still thoughtful. 'But if he knew you, and recognized – or found out about – the flag of Sluis on the ship ... You must tell Lord Francis. He needs to be aware in case Hugh tells his uncle, and Lord Soulsby tells ...'

She broke off before uttering the name. Her fingers were picking absently at the leather binding of the book now on her lap. Shadow, curled at her feet all this time, stirred and stood, stretched, then nuzzled at her hands as though for reassurance. But whose? The gesture sparked memories of my own hound, her sister Murrey.

As I watched, lost in that remembrance, Alys spoke again. To my surprise, her words were hesitant.

'When you do speak to him ... Lord Francis will listen to you, I'm sure ... And Edward will too. For all you say that you are his servant, I know you have become close.' Had we? I was not so certain. 'When you speak to him – Lord Francis, I mean – will you plead my case for accompanying you all to Dublin?'

'You? To Dublin?'

For all the surprise that rang in my voice, there was less in my heart. Alys, I knew, would hate to be left behind.

'Yes. Of course. There's little enough for me here once you've gone. And I – I have never seen Ireland. Though my father served King Edward there before I was born. In fact, it is where my parents met.' Her words were building a case for travelling even as they tripped from her lips. And the next ones clinched it for me.

'And if Hugh did see me – did recognize me at Lowestoft – his uncle will now guess where I am. I don't want Lord Soulsby – or Dame Grey – sending word to Duchess Margaret to demand I be returned to them.'

9

Eyes of a Hawk

To my amazement, Lord Francis did listen to me with close attention while I related my tale – and Alys's plea along with it.

I had knocked at the door of his chamber after supper. As he ushered me in, several freshly opened letters were clasped in his hand.

'If young Hugh did recognize you,' he said as I finished speaking, 'and maybe also me – then told his uncle, who told ... well, that might account for some of this.' He brandished the letters but offered no further explanation. 'Though Tudor – and his mother, no doubt – they have spies everywhere. My movements have not gone unobserved and unreported this past year or more. They may well have a good picture of our intentions already.'

The unease that had been growing since my conversation with Alys drained away. My delay in speaking appeared not to be a problem. But there was still the other matter to pursue.

'And Alys, my lord?'

'She truly wants to go to Ireland?' To my surprise a small smile touched his lips.

'She says so.'

'Perhaps it would not be a bad thing. She is brave enough for the voyage – has journeyed among rough soldiers and sailors before.' His eyes travelled up and down my Burgundian finery, the curve of his lips growing. 'Not to mention Plantagenet princes and their men incognito. And I rather suspect Edward would like her to go.'

'My lord?'

He must have seen puzzlement on my face or heard it in my voice.

'Oh, come, Matthew. You are not blind. You have seen them together. Or do I imagine that he brightens when she enters the room? That he hangs on her words like a faithful hound?'

'My lord, I —'

My speech floundered as I scoured my memory. It was true I rarely saw Alys and Edward together, but when I did ...

'I suppose it may be so. He is less ... he has perhaps been less melancholy since we returned from England. Despite the news of Lord Lincoln. But – but I don't think she feels the same.'

Warmth rushed into my face as the words tumbled out, and I cursed inside. Lord Francis, however, showed no sign of noticing. He laid down the letters among others scattered upon the table where he had been working when I entered.

'I'm glad to hear you say that, Matthew. I thought as much too. And I would not wish to encourage her – or them – in this. When Edward is king, he will need to marry – and it will be best for everyone that he seeks abroad for a wife. To secure a political alliance. As perhaps his father should have done. We might not have been in this situation if he had, and Richard ...'

His words trailed off and he turned his head away as he often did when he mentioned his old friend. As he began to speak once more, his voice was muffled, as though from a great distance.

'Many things might have been different. Richard might have lived out his life serving his brother as he did for so many years. And I – I might not have to carry the burden of my decision with me everywhere.'

A heartbeat's pause.

'I think of him every day. Of that moment when the mêlée broke. Whether there was anything more I could have done. But I knew then I could not save him – that he was dead already. That to fight my way back to where he lay would have been self-slaughter. Suicide. It's a mortal sin – to kill oneself. And he would not have wished me to endanger my immortal soul.'

Silence reigned for some moments. I could say nothing in comfort. I knew I too had failed my king on that day – although what I had done afterwards had perhaps made some amends. Despite all Lord Francis's actions since, it was clear he had made no peace with himself.

But he shook himself, almost like a dog that has just awoken, and when he spoke again, his tone was not so dark.

'But now we must do what we can for his nephew. All of us. It is what Richard would have wanted. And so long as the duchess agrees, that may include Alys. She has not had an easy time of it either, since …' He shied away from the memory again. 'It may be that a change of scene in Dublin will do them both some good. And perhaps she can also keep an eye on you two young hotheads.'

'Hotheads, my lord?' Surely he didn't mean Edward and me?

Though his eyes were still shadowed, his faint smile returned.

'Do not take it amiss, Matthew. Maybe that is an exaggeration. If it were young Richard, now – or his cousin George, from what I've seen of that little ruffian since we arrived – if it were either of them, I might well have more cause to worry. Perhaps, instead, I should have said you, Matthew, can do me the service of keeping a watchful eye on our new king and his young lady. Even if she has no notion of being any such thing.'

Duchess Margaret did not share his lordship's light-hearted view of any growing friendship between Edward and Alys. She gave her consent to Alys joining the company heading soon to Dublin but appeared less than happy about the idea. When the two of them were in her presence, her eyes watched them as though she were one of the falcons perched in her extensive mews. And if they dared speak to one another, she would swoop down upon them to ensure their conversation was appropriate.

Edward didn't notice – perhaps because he had spent longer at his aunt's court and was not surprised by abrupt changes in her behaviour. But Alys bridled at the interference.

'It's as though I've done something to offend her,' she complained to me one day when we ourselves happened to be alone. 'I can't speak to Edward at all without her pouncing upon us. I wouldn't mind so much, but Richard and George do snigger so and point at me behind her back every time it happens. To be the butt of their jokes so often is becoming tiresome.'

If she was not aware what the issue was, I doubted it was my place to tell her. So I only tried to soothe her annoyance.

'It won't be for much longer, if you're going to Ireland. And I hear Richard will be sent away soon, in case Tudor's agents seek him once we are there. George – well, George wouldn't dare to bait you without his cousin around. You know he goes in fear of Edward, and is only brave enough when Richard eggs him on.'

'I suppose he is only young,' she admitted, 'nine or ten at most. And has never had the guiding hand of a father.'

'They've struck up such a friendship since you left last year. George will miss Richard when he leaves.'

'Perhaps it will not be for so very long.' Her sympathy for the boys appeared to drive away her irritation. 'When Edward regains his throne, Richard will return to England too – and perhaps George will join them. The duchess has shown him great favour since his father was executed, but Edward says he would prefer all his cousins to be about him in England – even those who are only natural sons of their father, like George.'

'You mean, as King Richard sent his natural son to live at Sheriff Hutton with little Ed? Half-brothers together?'

I cast my mind back to those days after I had left Yorkshire – when life had also changed for those still at

Middleham Castle. When little Ed had become Prince of Wales and been given his own household at a castle nearer York, with the Earl of Lincoln to help him run the new Council of the North. Before Ed —

I thrust my thoughts away from my poor dead friend, towards his illegitimate brother.

'John was his name, wasn't it?'

'Yes – John of Gloucester. He was several years older than Ed. He was as tall and strong as … well, as Ed wasn't tall and strong. And there was also his sister – or half-sister, I think. Katherine. I wonder what happened to them after —'

A shadow darkened her eyes, before I saw her grasp her own thoughts too and force them in a different direction.

'Perhaps Edward will treat them well too when he becomes king – they're also his cousins after all. And, of course, there's George's half-brother – Edward, my lord of Clarence's true-born son.'

'Wasn't he at Sheriff Hutton as well?'

'Yes. But I gather Tudor now keeps him in prison in the Tower of London. He fears the people may rise in rebellion to support him if he is free.'

'What – even though his father was attainted for treason?' I asked, trying to recall all I had learned of the Duke of Clarence's disloyalty to old King Edward many years before. 'Surely that means he can't inherit the throne.'

'And he's only about eleven. You wouldn't expect he'd be much of a threat.'

'Tudor seems almost to fear his own shadow.' But my laugh was hollow.

'It may be because he is another Earl of Warwick,' Alys said. 'The Kingmaker's name still stirs the hearts of many people, despite his later treachery against King Edward. This boy may only be his grandson, but …'

'Do you think those people will rise also in support of our Edward?'

'Perhaps.' After her time in England, her idea of the mood of its people was clearer than any we could glean in faraway Flanders. 'But I imagine it's far from certain. I have to sound reassuring when Edward talks about it, for fear he will lose heart for all that is ahead – or doubt that he can claim his throne again. Lady Tyrell, Lord Francis, and —' she hesitated, 'and Elizabeth have asked me to encourage him.'

'Elizabeth?' Her mention of the name stunned me. 'His sister? The new queen?'

'She isn't queen yet,' Alys retorted, 'and may never be. Tudor has so far refused to have her crowned. As though he truly believes he need not rely on her royal ancestry – her father's family – to bolster his claim to the throne. But, while some people may resign themselves to his rule, others – well, others don't take kindly to his arrogance.'

'And Elizabeth herself?'

I was curious. I had only met the lady – Princess Elizabeth as she was then – very briefly at her father's court and did not know her. Even from Edward I had learned little, as he had rarely spent time with her as a boy. He had lived mostly with his uncle Rivers in Ludlow, while she remained at court with their parents. But she had also undergone trials in recent years, buffeted by the harsh winds of fortune. Spurned in marriage by a French prince. Declared illegitimate by Parliament after her father's death. That death itself, of a man she had appeared close to. Months spent in sanctuary where her mother fled when her plotting had failed. Hopes of a longed-for betrothal to a Portuguese duke dashed by her uncle's defeat in battle. Then marriage to the man who had stolen the throne – a man she had never met before. In none of this had she had much say.

'Elizabeth says little of it all – in her letters to me, at least,' said Alys. 'I think she dare not let herself hope that her life can change now in any real way – that she does not have to live out all her days as the wife of the usurper, whether or not she is mother to his child.'

The downright disgust on her face might have been comical had the reason for it not been so serious. I smothered the smile that threatened to betray me as she went on, 'But she wishes her brother well.'

'So she knows he still lives?'

'Elen has taken letters between us, and I have told her – well, not quite everything of course, but enough. She's terrified that Tudor will find him and Richard, and send men to kill them – for all they are her brothers. She's told me she doesn't wish to know where they are, so she need not lie if he asks her – but that I am to send Edward her messages of support.'

She sighed. 'There is much love among the people for her and her family still, if not for their mother. And if Tudor doesn't soon make her his queen, they may start to show their unhappiness.'

My mind snapped back to what Duchess Margaret had said about marriages being annulled. Perhaps Elizabeth had similar ideas. Yet I knew Alys could not have received word from her friend since she had given birth to her son, as Elen had been sent to Gipping before her lying-in. Might that have made a difference? Would the arrival of baby Arthur – heir to Henry Tudor and the beginning of what the usurper hoped would be a new dynasty – have changed Lady Elizabeth's mind? And what influence would that have on Edward and his still-uncertain plans?

10

Greyfriars

No word came from England in the following days to answer any of my questions. Meanwhile the date of our departure for Ireland drew ever closer.

Edward now had me running errands all over town in preparation for the journey and arrival in a new city. He must wear only the most recent continental fashions to impress his new allies and carry the best-crafted weapons his aunt's money could buy – fit to match his magnificent sword with the scrollwork inscription that I now knew had been presented to him by his father long ago. And the best armourer in Flanders had spent weeks hammering and riveting the most splendid suit of plate mail that had ever been seen in all the emperor's many lands.

One day I was returning from collecting not one, not two, but three pairs of the finest tooled leather boots to be had in the whole of the Low Countries, when a liveried servant caught me as I was about to re-enter the palace.

'Meneer Wansford? Her Grace wishes to speak with you.'

I followed him dutifully. To my surprise, he led me not through the huge metal-shod doors of the duchess's residence, but back along the street I had just traversed, across the vast market square, with its busy traffic of wagons, mules and hollering farmers from out of town, and through winding backstreets until we reached the outer wall of an ancient priory. The spear-like spire of the nearby St Rombald's Cathedral towered above us, still part-shrouded with wooden scaffolding and with the stonemasons tiny dots like far-off birds as they scrambled about their work under sullen, rain-filled clouds.

An elderly servant waved us through the plain wooden doors of the priory and into the gloom of its tall-pillared church. I was glad to gain its shelter as the first drops of the promised downpour spattered my face and best livery.

Few worshippers were within at this time of day, between services as it was, so I spied Duchess Margaret without difficulty – in the choir close to the high altar, accompanied by only a few attendants. I hung back, not wishing to disturb her devotions, but the servant ushered me forwards. This great lady, clad in the costliest velvets, silks and jewels, was kneeling on the cold, grey stone flags, her head bowed almost to the floor.

I watched, silent, from the shadow of a column. Soon she pushed herself up to her feet, brushing away the attentions of her attendants trying to help. Her hands clutched a black-jewelled rosary, her fingers flicking its beads along in well-worn habit, even as the servant announced me and her eyes sought me out.

'Ah, Master Wansford. My people have found you at last.'

I bowed low to her.

'My apologies, Your Grace. I had no idea they were seeking me or I would have returned sooner.'

'No matter. No doubt you were on an errand of highest importance for my nephew.' A smile curved her shapely mouth, but as so often, no glimmer of laughter shone in her eyes.

I bowed again in assent. I had no need to speak. It was well known throughout the palace household that Edward now kept me busy on his affairs almost from daybreak to day's end. Gone were my opportunities for reading in the pleasure ground – even had the weather permitted it. The bright but chill days after our return from England had given way to the grey blustery conditions of early winter, and I was daily doing my best not to imagine what might be awaiting us on our coming sea voyage.

The duchess at least was well prepared to travel back to her palace – a servant was hovering with a voluminous hooded mantle ready to envelop her. But now she waved that aside as she had all attempts to assist her as she rose. I do not think I had ever known a lady so determined to rebuff all well-meaning attentions.

'We shall remain here for a moment,' she said to her attendants, taking my elbow and steering me away from them, back into the choir. 'I have one or two things to say to you, Master Wansford.'

Yet some minutes passed before she spoke again.

I stood mute, by her side, as she gazed at the high altar before us, the gold of its immense cross shimmering despite the dim light, and up at the expanse of stained glass above. The colours of the biblical scenes were for once dull on this most overcast of days. Never before had the storm clouds gathered above Noah's ark appeared so ominous.

'Take care of my nephew for me, Master Wansford.'

Her voice was as cool as the grey sky that loomed outside. But as I looked now at her face, her eyes were glistening, not with their usual ice, but something softer.

'It is perhaps a rash task that he has taken upon himself. I have encouraged him in it, but I'm uncertain whether his decision – or mine not to refuse him – is wholly wise. He will need every friend around him to support him.'

'Of course, Your Grace,' I replied. 'I shall do everything I can within my power.'

'Will that be enough, I wonder?'

My cheeks flushed warm at her words, quiet and distracted though they were, and despite the gloom in the church, she must have seen my colour rise.

She placed a hand upon the blue sleeve of my doublet.

'Forgive me, Matthew. It is not you I doubt. You have been a good and loyal friend to Edward, and I'm sure you will continue to serve him well. But ... but what faces him is an immense undertaking. His father – my brother – found success, twice, in similar endeavours against huge odds, winning, then later regaining, his throne. But young Edward is a very different person. He has had a different life, different training.'

His uncle's words at Stony Stratford, three long years ago, came back to me now – his voice not unlike his sister's deep tones: 'Perhaps young Edward has been too softly brought up. At only a few years older, his father had lost his own father and fought to win his crown at Towton. I wonder whether this boy would be able to face such troubles as those.'

Edward would hate to hear such misgivings about his abilities, his determination – about whether he could live up to his Plantagenet forebears. No wonder Alys had been charged with encouraging him.

The duchess's thoughts must have been running along similar lines.

'I remember my brother Richard, before he became king, writing to me of Edward and his worries about him. He felt the boy's Woodville blood and his training with Earl Rivers had not fitted him well to be king in a still-troubled country – certainly not at such a young age.'

Her eyes narrowed as she considered me, standing still beside her.

'Yet we forget how little you young people know – of why we older ones cannot forgive those who supported the Lancastrians. They not only denied my father his proper claim to the kingdom, but murdered him and my brother Edmund in cold blood. Edmund was only seventeen – just three years older than I was. Only a year older than Edward is now.'

I listened to her talk of events so long ago, years before I was born. It was true – I had forgotten that old King Edward, when he wed Elizabeth Woodville, had married a member of a Lancastrian family – natural enemies to his own House of York in the civil war that had raged in those times. For all Henry Tudor's trumpeting of his marriage to Elizabeth of York, his was not the first such union of the two houses – or at least, of their supporters.

'And then,' Her Grace continued, 'after years of peace, the little that was left of the Lancastrian line – that disinherited Tudor branch – returned. To take advantage of the turmoil and uncertainty caused by my brother Edward's imprudent marriage – or marriages. Hoping to overturn the established order and destroy the last remnants of the glorious House of York.'

She shook her head, gazing down now at the flagstones beneath our feet, her face veiled by the lace falling gently from her tall hennin.

'I thank you for what you told me, Matthew – about the good friars of Leicester and their treatment of my brother Richard. That they gave him the right and proper burial that Tudor would likely have denied him, even if it was hasty. When our Good Lord sees fit to gather me to him, I have left instructions that I wish to be buried here –' I heard the soft tap of her shoe on the hard stone beneath her skirts, 'here, in the same place, in the choir within this their sister church in Mechelen – in memory of him.'

Her sigh barely reached my ears, despite the near silence in the church. But in an instant her voice rallied, as though moving on after overcoming a troublesome obstacle.

'But my nephew Edward ... in the here and now ... Richard did what he felt was best to deal with the mess our brother Edward left behind him – the stain of illegitimacy, the overweening ambition of the Woodvilles and so many others. Also he genuinely believed it was better for England to be governed by a grown man – a proven general and administrator – rather than by an untested boy, especially one ruled by his mother's jumped-up family. I gave him my support then. Now I will give it to young Edward. Tudor will recognize his mistake in making the boys legitimate again along with their sister. Even if that means I must wink at their father's indiscretions.'

She fell silent a moment, before speaking again.

'In a few days you will travel to Ireland. I hope you may have an easy journey of it and through Lord Lovell's careful deception, evade the notice of Tudor. You should, God willing, be there in good time to celebrate Yuletide.'

Her eyes slipped towards mine. I stifled the smile nudging my lips at the thought of the coming festivities.

'You will all find Dublin very different to here and, though the Kildares have long been friends to the House of York, Edward will have to work hard to gain their assistance in any meaningful way. Invasions of Ireland have been launched from England before, but I doubt Tudor will be enticed to do that at this still-precarious stage of his reign. More likely Edward will have to cross the sea again in order to meet him in battle in England.'

Her gaze rose again to the window depicting the storm-tossed Noah's ark, then returned to my face.

'I will send what troops I can once we are assured that Kildare is on our side, and perhaps our endeavour will meet with success. Meanwhile I trust you and Viscount Lovell will give him your full support.'

'Of course, Your Grace,' I said once more, with a bow. I could say nothing else. And I was awed she had joined my name with that of Lord Francis in this way.

Duchess Margaret's face altered subtly, her sombreness shifting to – I wasn't sure. Was it indulgence?

'And that young tearaway Alys Langdown. Arriving here uninvited, then demanding to travel to Ireland with you all! She is a young lady with a mind of her own. It would not have been tolerated when I was a girl. Yet, perhaps she will look after you all ...'

Those words, though strangely soft-spoken, rang in my ears only days later as our company at last set off from the palace on the first leg of our journey.

It was a quiet parting, early in the morning, under a forbidding muster of winter rainclouds. Gathered in the stableyard, along with body servants and a detachment of men-at-arms, were Edward, Lord Francis, the Mallary brothers, Alys, a young maid assigned to her by the duchess, two more emissaries and me. Alys, of course, insisted she would ride alongside the gentlemen, rather than in the carriage the duchess provided, and as we all assembled, at the first opportunity, she complained to me that the maid was unnecessary.

'I had no maid with me when we travelled from England before – either time.'

'Duchess Margaret only wishes to help you,' I soothed, knowing well Alys wouldn't heed my words. 'Her Grace is concerned about you. That ...'

'That what?'

What was it exactly the duchess had hinted? And should I have even started to say it?

I stumbled over my words.

'That you may be a ... a little, er, reckless at times – not perhaps always the lady you should be.'

She snorted – perhaps proving the point.

'I will be my own self – not confined by what is expected of me. Perhaps once ... But now ... now there are more important things than being ladylike and demure and preparing ... well, preparing for some marriage that may – I hope – never happen.'

'Never?' Her declaration shocked me. 'Not Ralph, of course, not now. But never?'

Her keen green eyes held mine, their gaze steady.

'We can never know the future, Matt, but at this moment ... I can think of no one I would consider marrying, and no circumstances when ... Not while I have the friendship and protection of such powerful ladies.'

'But if Duchess Margaret wished —?'

'Don't forget – I am not her ward.'

'No, but —'

'Dame Grey is my guardian, Matt. She controls my fortune, if not my person. And though I may live among Duchess Margaret's household, Her Grace has no legal power over me. She cannot force me to wed. And at present she has no reason to bow to Dame Grey's wishes either. I am safe from marriage for the time being.'

As I digested what she had said, silenced by her determination, she prodded me, gesturing to where Edward was taking leave of his younger brother a few feet away.

'Richard is another matter,' she whispered with a smile. 'He must do Her Grace's bidding. Dame Grey has no power over him at all, it seems, though she is his mother.'

The duchess had bid farewell to the party in her audience chamber, but had allowed Richard to accompany us to the stableyard to send us on our way. His still-boyish voice was running on, while Edward, unspeaking, gazed down at him from atop Storm, richly caparisoned now in murrey and blue as befitted a Yorkist king's horse.

'They say I may go to Portugal or Spain on some merchant ship, disguised as an ordinary passenger to escape Tudor's notice – just like you will. Or perhaps to the court of Duke Maximilian or the emperor himself. Of course, Aunt Margaret has not said – nor whether George will come with me. She says it's safer if I – and you – do not know yet. But I will write, Ned, as often as I am able – to tell you how I am and of all that I do.'

Edward nodded but his mouth remained tight closed as though he found it difficult to respond.

'And will you write to me too? When you can? When you are not feasting with Irish lords or marching on London to smite the usurper?'

At that, Edward's lips curved slightly and he leant down to grasp his brother by the shoulder.

'I will, Dickon, when I have time. I promise. But, don't forget, letters will not travel easily or quickly from Ireland to here. Do not expect to hear from me often or soon.'

'I know,' Richard responded stoutly. 'But I hope your crossing will be swift and comfortable, despite the season. Let me hear tell of it as soon as you arrive.'

11

Storm

Richard's hopes and any prayers he may have offered up were to little avail over the coming days.

The Flemish sailors told me that, in fair weather, with a good wind, the voyage could take little more than a week. Some had made the journey many times, plying their master's trade through the English Channel, risking the attentions of pirates, then turning into wilder seas on the final phase of the journey towards Ireland. They had warned us that those last days often brought rough conditions, even in summer months.

Yet not one had ever known seas like those we encountered in those December days. For once, for the first time in all my journeyings, these experienced sailors had no time or energy or desire to mock and laugh at their passengers who were less seasoned or less hardy travellers.

The gales that met our sturdy merchant carrack as it slipped out of the sheltered harbour of Sluis and along the Flemish coast were nothing like those that struck later in the voyage, but even then, the ship's captain, a trusted Fleming with a good command of English, spoke of turning back.

'Or at least into a nearby port, my lord, where we can wait for calmer seas,' I overheard him say to Lord Francis.

But Lord Francis saw no reason to delay. Edward had found his sea legs and was impatient to be on his way, Alys and the Burgundian emissaries were cheerful enough (my own feelings were not consulted and were of no consequence to anyone), and the distress and seasickness of a lady's maid and a few men-at-arms who had barely travelled beyond Mechelen's town walls were not viewed as a problem. So Captain van Hecke was persuaded to push on, and a day or two later we sailed into the more open waters of the Channel beyond the narrow Calais strait.

We enjoyed a day of relative tranquillity as we cruised south within sight of the high stone walls and wave-dashed bastions of Calais, this last English town on the mainland of France – so often now its enemy. But before the sun had risen far the next morning, an immense bank of clouds was racing to overtake it, and by noon had swallowed it in its deep black maw. As the world about us darkened, a sudden vicious wind began to snap at the sails and the sea to roll in mighty waves.

'Get below decks, my lords,' Captain van Hecke urged those of us who remained above. 'You will be best out of this weather – and out of the way of my men who have to deal with it.'

We reeled across the now-swaying deck towards the captain's cabin. As the only lady on the ship, Alys, with her maid, had been the honoured guest there since we first came aboard, while the captain had taken instead a hammock alongside his men. The largest, finest cabin nestled within the aftercastle, it served as a communal space for us below decks, on this merchant ship unaccustomed to passengers.

Though Edward and one of the emissaries had gone below earlier, at the first signs of a pitching sea, they were now nowhere to be seen. All that met my eyes were servants scurrying here and there about the room, retrieving and fastening down anything that was loose. As we entered, a stout oaken chest slid towards us across the sloping timber floor, pursued by two men. They arrested it before it crushed us, lifted it up and swept it out the doorway.

Alys looked at me, eyes wide, clutching on to the door jamb to steady herself as the ship rocked again. Her maid, Berthe, was clinging on to the side of a bunk, wailing.

'All your clothes, my lady! They've taken them!'

'That chest! It was what Her Grace sent with me.'

'They'll stow it safely away,' I reassured her. 'I'm sure everything will be fine.'

'But it could have killed us,' she protested. 'I said I would be happy with just a bundle.'

'The chest isn't that big,' I said, craning to watch the men's unsteady progress away along the passage. 'Though it does look as though it would hurt if it hit us. Anyway, you'll need fine gowns and linens when we get to Ireland.'

'If we get to Ireland,' she fired back. 'If this gale gets worse, perhaps we may not. But at least I wouldn't have to worry about dressing up then.'

Before I could respond to her talk of shipwreck, Lord Francis came in behind us, with the two emissaries.

'Edward has retired to our cabin,' he told us. 'He says he's well, but if there is food, we should take him some before the storm really strikes.'

Sailors I'd met with on previous voyages had advised eating a good meal to calm the belly before rough weather hit. The servants rustled one up now and as they served my companions, I thrust away Alys's misgivings of disaster and carried a portion through to Edward, in the tiny cabin we shared with Lord Francis and the Burgundians. He was sitting on the edge of his bunk, his lips white-rimmed as though his stomach already juddered, like the cabin walls themselves. But he only took the food from me and dismissed me and my concerns with a wave of his hand.

As I returned to the captain's cabin, bracing myself against the timber walls of the dark undulating passageway, one of the emissaries pushed his way past me. He stumbled back towards our cabin, one hand clamped to his mouth and a slop bucket clenched in the other.

I stepped inside the chamber. Alys and Lord Francis were picking at their own food, but as the servant slapped a mess of cold pottage on to his trencher, the remaining emissary swallowed hard, clapped a hand to his own mouth, mumbled an apology between its fingers and lurched away out of the door.

'Two down,' said Alys. Then her eyes slipped to where Berthe was scuttling into the corner, hugging another bucket to herself. As the maid hunched over it with a moan, Alys averted her gaze. 'Or is that three?'

Although she said it with a smile, her own cheeks had now drained to a greyish-white shade I had never seen before.

Lord Francis stood up, still holding his food, listing a little to one side with the movement of the floor.

'Matthew, I think we should be away to our own cabin and leave the ladies in peace. My lady.'

He bowed to her and collecting the emissary's discarded trencher in his free hand, hustled me out of the doorway.

'Here, take this.'

He thrust the trencher into my waiting hands, before leaning back to tug the door to. But he was not quick enough to block the briefest glimpse of Alys tottering after Berthe and doubling up over the bucket herself.

We made our hesitant way back towards our cabin, managing perhaps one pace forward to one or more sideways or backwards as the rocking of the ship increased, keeping hold of our trenchers with difficulty. Tensing himself against the slope of the passageway, Lord Francis shoved open the door. A wave of groans and retching and a tide of stinking air rolled towards us from all three inmates, now lying prone upon their bunks.

His lordship pulled the door closed again before turning to me.

'Perhaps we would do well to eat before we enter.'

The reek that had blasted us had made my own insides wobble, and the greyish hue of his lordship's face hinted he had not escaped either. But I did my best to follow his example and force the thick stew down my gullet to settle my stomach, though its bland taste was overpowered always by the stench all around us. I also strove to turn my thoughts from Alys's forebodings. We voyaged in a well-built ship, well-captained and crewed. Surely all would be well.

We could not long avoid our companions and their plight. Everywhere about the ship we were faced with the growing violence of the storm, the surging and tossing of the hammocks, timber walls and decks, and more and more seasickness among soldiers, servants and even the sailors. Before many hours had passed, Lord Francis made our excuses to those hardier men with whom we had holed up, and we crept back to our tiny cabin, where he climbed shakily into his bunk.

Until that time, my belly was still holding steady, and I planned to forage later for food for my supper. But once the first rainbow arc of vomit had looped into his lordship's slop bucket, and the constant retching of all my companions snaked into my now-queasy brain, and the throat-catching stench from the splattered contents of the soon-overturned pails settled about us, I knew it was now or never. I swung out of my bunk and, hanging on to any handhold I could, dragged myself on to the deck.

But as I thrust myself out into the battering wind and dashing rain, and saw the thrashing of the towering waves beyond the side, and felt the tilting of the deck to one side then the other, my head began to spin and I found myself clinging on to the lurching side-rail of the ship. Alongside me hunched a raw young sailor, whose green-tinged face I knew mirrored my own as he turned it towards the seething waves. We both hurled what remained of our last meal into the swirling wind and scourging spray, with no strength left even to care when it was flung back into our own faces.

But he, and all the sailors, still had their tasks to perform, however their heads and insides might roil with the gargantuan swell of the sea. After I crawled back to my bunk, picking my way across the slippery, spew-strewn cabin floor and collapsing upon the thin mattress, I dared not dwell, during the terrible, chaotic, storm-filled days that followed, on how any could climb the rigging or furl the heavy canvas sails or perform any other job that might be required of them to stop the ship truly being wrecked. Those of us with no jobs to do – beyond tending to what were now Edward's few wants, when he could not eat, barely drank and certainly had no thought for fashionable clothes or weapons – could at least lie quiet in our bunks, our eyes closed against the pitching of our world in this raging tempest.

In my sickness and exhaustion, I soon lost count of the days and nights that passed before I saw anything or anyone beyond the four foul walls of the cabin, let alone glimpsed the sickly glow of the thundery sky again or breathed the fresh salt air upon the deck. But at long last, the heaving of the world around me lessened, the whirlpools in my head ceased their spinning, and the greenish hue of Edward's cheeks slowly faded, and one afternoon I hauled myself up a narrow ladder and scrambled through the hatch, and stood once more upon the freshly scrubbed deck of the aftercastle.

High above, black tatters of clouds scudded across the still-menacing sky, and rain lashed my too-warm face. The storm whipped at the ship still, but it was clear as I stood on my vantage point high in its stern that the worst was past. The cannon chained to the deck here only creaked softly now as its wheels shifted in the motion of the ship – even as my stomach still shifted a little. About me, sailors, soaked through and blue-edged with the cold of the winter afternoon, nodded to me as they went about their work. Their pinched faces told of their recent hardships with no need for words. It would be some time before snatches of song were the background to their tasks again.

Hours later, brands blazed against the black of the night sky and the gale no longer tore at the sails. Roasting meat spat and crisped above the coals of braziers close to the main mast, and the rich aroma brought the water springing in my mouth and rumbles of hunger in my belly for the first time in what seemed a lifetime. Crew and passengers drew together to cluster about the approaching dinner, the hum of conversation and scraps of laughter erupted again at last, and pasty features and drained eyes reflected the colours and glints of the flames. From the forecastle the lilting notes of a sailor's pipe drifted across the growing gathering, and deep inside me tugged a desire I had not felt in many months, a wish that I had my old lute to hand. After the trauma of past days, offering up a song of thanks for our deliverance would have been fitting.

Only when the trenchers of succulent mutton had been passed out, and my teeth had torn wolfishly at my first food for days, did Alys at last emerge from the captain's quarters, trailed as ever by Shadow. Captain van Hecke greeted her courteously and guided her through the parting waves of his sailors to warm herself by a brazier. Her smile when her eyes alighted on me was listless, not the usual quick flash, and her cheeks were pale and thin.

I collected another hard biscuit and slab of roasted flesh from the sailor tending the nearest fire – himself a boy younger than I, with huge dark eyes in his wasted face – and made my way across to where she stood, hunched beneath her thick fur mantle, a farewell gift from Duchess Margaret. She murmured her thanks as I handed her the steaming food, and then again when I returned from a brief search, bearing an empty barrel for her to use as a stool.

'How are you, Alys? I've not seen you since the storm began.'

'I've felt better,' she said, as she perched on her makeshift seat, something of her normal manner returning. It would perhaps be a while before her colour did, for all she was now tearing at the meat as I had a few minutes earlier. She swallowed a mouthful or two, and flicked a piece into Shadow's eagerly waiting mouth, before raising her eyes to me again.

'It's good to be out of that foetid cabin at last. Not that I was not grateful to be in there, with only two of us to worry about. How is Edward? And Lord Francis?'

'Well enough, I thank you,' came his lordship's voice from the darkness behind her. His tall, lean figure emerged into the pool of light cast by the nearest brand. Beyond him, two smaller shapes, also swathed in cloaks, were making their way back towards the doorway into the aftercastle. They were trailed by a sailor bearing a tray of meat and wooden cups from which steam plumed into the night-time breeze. I recognized the two Burgundians in the light of a torch fixed above the doorway as they dipped their heads beneath it.

Turning back towards the fire, I caught Lord Francis watching me.

'Edward, however, is not so well,' he said, then raised his hand as I moved to leave. 'No, do not go to him, Matthew. Stay and rest a while. He is but a little melancholy again. The seasickness and foul air and lack of food have taken their toll. Their excellencies offered to take him meat and drink and sit with him in the cabin a while, and I'm sure that will help.'

He squatted down by the brazier and rubbed his hands towards its glow as the captain bustled up with a hunk of roast mutton for him and cups of mulled ale for us all. As we supped and ate and supped again, and the voices of two or three sailors joined the pipe in a wistful song, Lord Francis spoke of Edward again.

'I think we must all be watchful in the days and weeks to come. Our young king in waiting is steadfast in his aim, but when adversity strikes … well, it may be that his confidence can be shaken. If he remains determined to pursue the throne, then we must do our utmost to help him steer the right course – or he may lead us all into dangerous waters.'

12

Dangerous Waters

The dangerous waters of our voyage didn't cease with the ending of the storm, though at first they were calm enough.

Next morning, soon after we had breakfasted, Alys and I were on deck again, leaning on the ship's rail. I was enjoying breathing in the cool clean air, but she was mainly complaining about her maid, Berthe.

'She says she does not believe the storm is over. She's convinced that every movement of the ship is caused by terrifying gales that will be the death of us all. And she insists her insides are still in such turmoil that she cannot even stand.'

She paused a moment, craning to see down to the water far below.

'The sea is not as still as a mill pond, but it's only a little choppy now. And she was happy to eat the food the cook took her last night. I suspect she just wants to lie abed for as long as she can.'

I found it difficult to blame Berthe for that wish. As my hands gripped the smooth wooden rail, I recalled too clearly the previous occasion I had done just that – when I and the young sailor had bid farewell to our last meals all those days ago. But Alys was right. Few white-tipped waves were in evidence below, and the ship was slicing through those with little speed. Its sails barely billowed in what breeze there was. The captain had ordered full canvas to be unfurled, and far above us, beneath the overcast sky, sailors were still scurrying about the rigging on all three masts, doing his bidding.

My eyes slipped down again to what lay before us. Our first sight of land for what seemed an age. Black cliffs reared up straight from the grey sea spray, from time to time inlets cut through them to reveal thin sandy beaches fringed with slopes of green, and small rocky islands were dotted here and there as far as I could see. It was a forbidding coastline, with no sign of human life anywhere. No cottages nestling in the sheltered coves, no fishing boats bobbing in tidy harbours, not even sheep or other livestock grazing upon the clifftops or on the grassy slopes leading up from the shore.

I shivered. It was so alien compared with the busy Flemish port towns to which I was now used, or even the gentle rolling coast around Lowestoft or the estuary of the great River Thames in London.

Footsteps scraped on the wooden planks of the deck and Edward stepped between us, also resting his hands on the rail.

'Not a welcome sight,' were his first words after greeting us and responding to Alys's courteous query as to his health. 'Captain van Hecke told Lord Francis we were blown off course by the storm. So far indeed that this is the coast of Brittany.'

'Brittany!'

I had never travelled this way on my journeys with Master Ashley, and had only heard of the place as the lair of Henry Tudor when he was in exile. But Alys, as ever, knew more.

'Then he was correct last night when he said the distant lights we saw were from the English islands?'

'Guernsey, he believes,' said Edward, naming what even I knew to be the second largest of this cluster of islands just off the Normandy coast, ruled still by England though they lay so close to the French mainland. 'Francis says we did well not to put in there. Tudor replaced the Yorkist captains with his own men as soon as he could. And though we may be travelling as simple passengers, not all will be easily fooled. Word might well get back to them, especially perhaps about the number of soldiers aboard. We would not wish to alert them to our journey.'

'Will we be long delayed?'

Edward shrugged.

'Long enough, I expect. But at least we did not run aground on those rocky headlands, and have not yet fallen into Tudor's hands or those of pirates. They say many such prowl these waters.'

That was not a notion to linger on, but were they both thinking as I did? That surely our good Lord would not send us further trials after those of the past days. Neither spoke as we all gazed out at the daunting shoreline slowly unfolding before us.

After a few moments of silence, I stole a sideways glance at Edward. As I had earlier observed of Alys, some colour had returned to his cheeks, but they were still gaunt and ashen in the grey light of day and his eyes hollowed. It would likely be some time before we were all recovered from our ordeal.

A shout in Flemish burst from above us.

'Hoy! Schip!'

The sailor on watch up on the main mast was pointing straight towards the shore. I turned my eyes again that way just as a ship's prow was edging round the nearest rocky islet. The very tip of its single mast jutted above the jagged summit and it must have been that the watchman had spotted.

As the ship sailed fully into view, at unexpected speed given the little wind that was blowing, I saw how much smaller it was than our own, both in height and length – and also why it was so swift. As well as its full sail, it was propelled by a row of oars on each side. Unlike any ship I had seen upon the seas, it resembled more the many barges upon the Thames, engaged in ferrying passengers from one bank to another or unloading cargo from larger ships to transport to shore.

Captain van Hecke hurried up to the ship's side, accompanied by two or three sailors. Lord Francis joined him a moment later.

'Well, Captain?' he asked, leaning on the rail alongside us.

The captain squinted towards the unknown vessel, his eyes almost disappearing in his tanned, lined face.

'Just a fisher boat or a local coasting ship, my lord. Many ply their trade hereabouts.'

Above, the watchman bawled again. Another ship, of a similar type, hove into view around the same tiny island.

The captain bent forward now, one hand shading his eyes though there was no sunshine to disrupt his sight.

'Two ships, no flag,' I heard him mutter in Flemish, then he pivoted to Lord Francis.

'I doubt they will trouble us, my lord, but I will muster my men in case.'

'I hear there are pirates in these parts, Captain,' Lord Francis shot back. 'We also have men-at-arms aboard. We must make ready for any danger.'

Captain van Hecke nodded and began issuing instructions to his men. They scattered to various parts of the ship, including to the forecastle where the Flemish soldiers were quartered.

Lord Francis turned his attention to us.

'You had best return to your cabins until we are sure all is well.'

Beside me Edward tensed, as though to refuse, but before he could speak, the captain butted in.

'Aye, sir – no arguments. It would be safest.'

'Captain!'

Captain van Hecke flinched at the curt rebuke in his lordship's voice, then bowed to both gentlemen.

'Begging pardon. I meant to say "Your Grace". 'Twas but a slip of the tongue. I intended no disrespect. But Your Grace and my lady should go below.'

To my surprise, Alys at once withdrew to the aftercastle, dragging Shadow by her collar, and disappeared within.

Edward, however, stood his ground.

'Nay, Captain. I will remain. If these ships present a threat, I shall face it.'

Lord Francis beheld him for an instant, as though sizing him up, then nodded and turned instead to me.

'And you will stay too, Matthew, if you please. We may need your help to speak with them if they approach us. I remember how fluent you are in many tongues.'

My brow gathered in a frown. 'But I don't speak Breton, my lord.'

'Do your best, Matt. I understand it is a little like Welsh.' The ghost of a smile hovered about his lips.

'But —'

He was no longer listening, having swung back towards Edward and the captain, so I swallowed my protest. I knew no Welsh either. Though I had heard it once, joined with what I had taken to be jeers in Breton, on a thronged street in Leicester more than a year before.

As I thrust away that sharp pain of remembrance, the captain was pointing over the side.

'They turn this way, my lord. Their ships manoeuvre more easily than ours in these waters. I think I see what they are about.'

The two ships had indeed changed course. The foremost had already overtaken us, so great was the speed of its oars dipping in and out of the shallow waves, and now it veered as though to sail in front of us. The second vessel was heading straight towards our side. Upon both decks, I could now see men assembled – and also the weapons they wielded.

'My lord,' I said in warning, 'they are armed. Crossbows and halberds.'

Lord Francis twisted round to Captain van Hecke. 'Pirates?'

The captain did not respond at once. He was barking orders again and sailors ran to shin up all three masts. Elsewhere, others were collecting weapons of their own from boxes on the deck and men-at-arms were emerging one after another from the forecastle doorway, buckling on their leather armour and fastening their sallets.

Several hauled themselves up ladders to the fore- and aftercastles and busied themselves about the cannons chained there.

Captain van Hecke swung back to his lordship.

'Aye, my lord, I believe so,' he at last said in reply. 'We cannot outrun them, so I have given orders to furl the sails. It is best to accept we must wait and face them rather than try to escape.'

'Will we face them and fight?' asked Edward. Did I detect a quaver in his voice? If so, it was no more, and likely less, than that in my gut.

'Nay, Your Grace,' returned the captain. 'I trust there will be no need of that. These ruffians usually want no more than a little money or some goods. I'm sure we shall satisfy them without the need for —'

But whatever he meant to say was cut short as something zipped past my ear, then a deep thunk resounded from behind.

A roar of laughter rolled over the ship's rail towards us.

The second ship was now no more than a few score paces away, side on to us and matching our speed, and among the cluster of guffawing men upon its deck, two held raised crossbows.

The noise I'd heard was the flight of a crossbow bolt shot towards us. Whirling round, I spied it, quivering still, stuck a man's height up the main mast. My heart thumped with fear at how close it had come to me.

'Matthew, get down!' cried his lordship.

My companions had all ducked before another bolt flew towards us. I was late to follow them, but lucky once more. This one missed me too, but one of the sailors descending from the rigging was not so fortunate. It struck him in the arm as he climbed and, with a shriek of pain, he plummeted the final feet down to the deck.

As his mates scuttled, heads down, to pull him to safety, another laugh rang from the ship, then a shout. The words were in French – broken but intelligible. Captain van Hecke, crouching as we all now were behind the thick timber side of the ship, said, 'They call to us to surrender.'

'Never,' declared Edward. Though his face had paled at the shock of the attack, his voice was firm.

'We do not need to,' said Lord Francis, as the poor French was yelled in our direction again. 'We can more than match them.'

The commander of the men-at-arms had joined us in our shelter and with a few words, Lord Francis gave him his orders. As the man ran, bent double, towards the forecastle to carry them out, a third holler came from the pirate ship.

This time its meaning was clear to us all. The words were in English, with scarcely a trace of accent.

'Surrender. We shall not harm you.'

Lord Francis and the captain exchanged glances and frowned.

'That sounded like —'

But before his lordship could finish, lightning flashed, a tremendous explosion rocked the air and smoke bellied from the forecastle. An instant later, the roar was echoed from the stern. The cannons fore and aft had been fired.

My head still ringing with the din, I watched the company of soldiers rise to their feet across the width of the deck and forecastle, then advance in one rank towards the side and front of the ship, as smoke from both cannons billowed up towards the clouds. Marching together in a single row, in their burnished jacks and sallets and with their arquebuses and crossbows raised, all wreathed about by vapour, they must have appeared to the pirates like an army of fiends emerging from hell.

An order was bellowed by the commander and half of the handgunners lifted their weapons. Another order and the crack of a score or more guns tore at my ears. Those men knelt to reload, while their fellows trained their weapons still upon our foes.

A moment of quiet. The smoke from the

arquebuses drifted through the now still air and tasted gritty upon my tongue.

No laughter now came from either of the smaller ships.

With one of our soldiers standing sturdy before me, his gun ready to fire, I dared crane my head around him and peep across the side-rail.

All three ships had come to a halt in the gently rolling water – our sails furled, their oars stilled. And I heard something shouted in an unknown language, followed by a crash and clatter as our attackers threw down their weapons as one, and then saw the hands of all raised above their heads in surrender.

Our commander bawled another order in Flemish and a dozen sailors picked themselves up from their refuges around the deck. They scrabbled around for ropes to tie to iron grappling hooks, and within minutes they had cast them to catch on to the side of the nearest ship and were hauling it closer alongside our own.

The helpless pirates remained unmoving while they were towed towards their intended victims. As they neared, I could see not one was bloodied or wounded in any way, and I spied the peppering of shot holes that had pierced the sails well above their heads.

But I also saw the terror still splashed across their faces.

13

Pirate!

All aboard our ship were back upon their feet, now the danger was passed. Sailors were lowering the immense anchor to keep us steady and others were tending to their injured comrade.

Amidst the activity, Edward and Lord Francis stood side by side, watching the enforced approach of the pirates. The contrast was stark between these gentlemen in their fine fashions and the still-ready men-at-arms in their sturdy armour and colourful livery, and the pitiful tatters worn by our one-time adversaries as they cowered upon their captive vessel. Pity and contempt were mingled in their lordships' expressions.

Lord Francis bent his head towards me.

'They may be Bretons and barely know the French of their own neighbours,' he said quietly, 'but one at least speaks English. Find him for me, Matthew, if you can, and we may deal with this matter.'

The grimace that slid across his face betrayed his distaste. He did not wish to sully himself by addressing such men in his own faultless French, so I must make the attempt.

I stepped past my stout protector up to the rail and peered down at those who were now our prisoners. Sullen faces stared up at me.

Clearing my throat, I spoke in what I hoped was an assured voice.

'Messieurs, nous sommes des seigneurs anglaises. Vous êtes nos prisonniers. Parlez-vous français ou anglais?'

Most of the wretched men on the deck below exchanged glances and shrugs, but one, a young brawny fellow, shoved his way to the front.

'I speak French and English too, sir, if that will help.'

He spoke with just a wisp of an accent. Clad in less ragged garments of homespun wool, he appeared a cut above the rest, yet he had not the bearing of their leader. Who he was and what to say next baffled me. I hesitated, and my relief was two-fold as Lord Francis took charge.

'Then it was you who called for our surrender just before the cannon fired? How is it you speak English?'

The man thrust out his chest.

'I am a true-born Englishman, sir – in my way.'

'You may address me as "my lord",' said Lord Francis, with no sharpness this time, only a trace of curiosity. 'As an Englishman, how come you to be in the company of Breton pirates? And can you speak for them?'

'I am an Islander, my lord. Guillaume Tournier, from Guernsey, and misfortune befell me there. I have been with these men near half a year, and I believe they will let me be their voice.'

'Then come aboard, Master Tournier, and we will talk.'

With a few words and gesticulations among his shipmates, it was agreed and before long Guillaume Tournier had inched his way across one of the taut ropes suspended between the ships and been heaved over the side-rail by our sailors. By this time seats had been placed on deck for Edward and Lord Francis, and an intriguing audience with the man ensued. We soon discovered the reason for his flight from his home.

'I see from your man there, my lord,' his eyes flicked my way, 'that you are loyal still to the memory of our good Yorkist King Edward.'

This was not difficult to discern, as I stood behind Edward resplendent in a new tunic of murrey and blue, embroidered with the white Yorkist rose and old King Edward's blaze of a sun in splendour, prepared for me before we sailed.

Lord Francis nodded in assent.

'Aye, and to his brother, our late King Richard of blessed memory. What of it?'

'So too am I and my friends, my lord.' He gestured towards the pirate ship. 'Not these Breton fisherfolk, but my people at home. And when the usurper, Tudor,' he spat upon the deck with relish, 'stole the crown, we did what we could against him.'

And he told us his sorry tale. Many who lived on the islands in the Channel, he said, had remained faithful to their Yorkist English overlords and done their best to hold out against the new regime and its royal French backers.

'But too many were imprisoned or hanged, and once our captains left the islands, first Sir Edward Brampton,' did I see Lord Francis's mouth twitch at the name? 'then Master Harliston, we had no focus for our revolt.'

'Those gentlemen are loyal Yorkists, are they not?' asked Edward.

'Aye,' said his lordship, his smile now unmistakeable. 'Good and true. And perhaps we shall hear more of them hereafter. But pray continue your story, Master Tournier.'

'Well, my lord,' the man went on, 'a friend and I did what we could. One night we ran up old King Richard's banner above the barracks as a call to arms. But my mate was caught and hanged by Tudor's new captain. I was lucky to get away to the mainland. That's how I fetched up with these lads.'

'And turned to a life of piracy,' put in Captain van Hecke gruffly. 'Their lordships should hang you – all – here and now.'

Guillaume threw himself to his knees before Lord Francis.

'I beg mercy, my lord, for me and my shipmates. They are but poor fishermen who take a chance now and again for a greater catch. Most ships we stop are unarmed coastal vessels—'

'Which is why they were not expecting men-at-arms today, then?' interrupted the captain. 'Perhaps that will be a lesson for them.'

'They don't have men or weapons enough to stand and fight, sir, if the shipmasters won't give them some silver or barrels of drink or fancy goods. They harm no one, only threaten—'

Captain van Hecke snorted. 'Tell that to my man there,' he said and waved his hand towards his injured sailor. Propped up against the main mast, the man was having his upper arm roughly bandaged.

'It is but a flesh wound,' said Lord Francis, who had checked on the man before seating himself. 'And he was only bruised in his fall.'

''Twas perhaps a lucky shot,' offered Guillaume.

'Not for him.'

But the captain held his peace as Edward raised his hand.

'Stand up, Master Tournier. We shall not punish you or your fellows, despite their reckless attack. You have shown us loyalty in your homeland and brought us welcome news of staunch support in that distant part of my realm. Rest assured I shall deal with Tudor's unjust captain when I reclaim my throne.'

Puzzlement was grappling with the relief etched on Guillaume's face as he climbed back to his feet.

'My lord?' he questioned. 'Your throne?'

'Aye, Master Tournier,' said Lord Francis. 'You stand before your rightful king. This is His Grace, King Edward. The fifth of that name, son of our late lord Edward the Fourth.'

I had to smother my smile at the sight this speech produced. Guillaume's features ran through so many emotions as his gaze travelled across the faces of all of us sitting and standing about him. In the end he gave up his effort to quell his astonishment and flung himself on his knees again, this time before Edward.

'Forgive me, Your Grace. I did not know you.'

'Why should you?' said Edward. 'We have never met before today – and you will not have seen my face on coins or portraits.'

'But, Your Grace … I thought … or rather, we thought … that you were dead. They said … I mean, the rumours …'

A cloud drifted across Edward's eyes, but in an instant he blinked it away.

'No matter. What you thought then is of no consequence. I am before you now. Your liege lord.' He thrust out his hand towards Guillaume. Upon its third finger a deep blue stone curved high above a wide gold ring. 'Will you give up your life of piracy to join us on our journey to wrest my crown back from Tudor? Will you be loyal to me as you were to my father?'

The man seized his hand eagerly and pressed the ring to his lips.

'Aye, Your Grace, I will. Gladly.'

As he released Edward's hand and backed away, bowing, over and again, in his gratitude, Lord Francis nodded in approval.

'Wisely done, Your Grace,' he said in a quiet tone.

With Captain van Hecke ordering those about us to return to their tasks, perhaps only I heard him, apart from Edward himself. And perhaps only I saw the squaring of our young king's shoulders at his words.

14

Landfall

In contrast to the first leg of our voyage, the second was quiet, as though our good Lord thought he had toyed enough with us and our ship and had moved on to other concerns.

My companions slowly recovered their healthful complexions and the injured sailor was soon about his work again, with only a black eye and bandage to tell of his late woe. And Guillaume Tournier settled into life on board ship alongside his new comrades. Before long he had redeemed himself with Captain van Hecke by revealing he was a journeyman blacksmith by trade. The captain set him to mending and making myriad items about the ship with the tools he lugged aboard with his bundle, and Lord Francis assured him there would be work aplenty when our voyage was over.

There was no repeat of the storm over the coming days, although the seas were indeed rough as we rounded the far corner of England into the Celtic Sea. Edward stayed mostly below decks then, as we were all advised to when the conditions changed, but his spirits rose once more as we neared our destination. More than two weeks had passed since our departure from Sluis before the blue misty mounds of distant hills first rose towards the west.

The ship put in for a short time at the sleepy port town of Wexford, from where a horseman was despatched north to Dublin to take word of Edward's imminent arrival. My fellow passengers and I were allowed a breather upon the grey-stone quayside, the locals eyeing us curiously as they went about their daily business.

Edward, with a gallant bow, offered his hand to help Alys step from the gangplank. I followed a few paces behind as they strolled together past the barrels, sacks, fishing nets and coils of rope littering the harbourside. Shadow nosed around everything, following any scent that caught her fancy.

One of the Burgundian gentlemen stumbled as he stepped ashore, to be caught by Lord Francis's courteous outstretched hand. I guessed the reason. After so long afloat, it was some minutes before the stone flags beneath my feet, the wood and plaster buildings edging the harbour, the church spire beyond, and even the clouds in the wintry blue vault above, ceased to wash back and forth, back and forth, as though the sea's constant motion continued here on land.

The horses we'd brought with us were also released at last from their confining stalls below decks. They skittered and clattered their way along the plank on to the quay, Storm among them, flinging up their heads at the touch of the chill breeze. Their grooms clung to their lead reins and calmed them with soothing hands and quiet words as they walked them about the harbour. Later, though, they exchanged curses in Flemish when the captain told them his brief business here was done and that they must return their charges to the ship. I knew how difficult our voyage had been for both the horses and their keepers. Though it should be no more than another day before we made landfall at our destination, I also had to fight my reluctance to board once more. Yet at least that evening we again ate newly baked bread, and the barrels of drinking water that was becoming brackish had been replenished with fresh.

We rode anchor that night well off from the shore, but the lights of a good-sized town twinkled in the darkness to the west. No moon shone and the stars were distant diamonds, obscured only by fleeting shreds of clouds driven by the breeze and the brooding black bulk of a headland on the northern skyline. In the morning we were roused by Captain van Hecke before daybreak and breakfasted on new bread and ale in the pearly pre-dawn glimmer, as the sailors busied themselves setting the sails for the final stage of our voyage.

The sun burst up over the sea behind the ship, a fiery orb flaring red-gold, and upon the main mast unfurled a magnificent banner. The royal standard – rampant lions, fleurs de lys, silver roses – rippled and blazed as it caught the early rays, shining red, gold, jewelled blue, as I had not seen it since a fateful high summer morning more than a year before. It was another specially commissioned gift from Duchess Margaret to her nephew. He stood now on the forecastle, majestic in his new armour and murrey and blue surcoat, as the ship sailed its stately way beneath the shadow of the great headland into the waiting harbour.

The men-at-arms and those sailors who could be spared from the tasks vital to our safe arrival formed a guard of honour for him. Their ranks were echoed, as we glided across the still waters towards them, by a welcome party of mail-clad soldiers standing to attention upon the quayside. A lone trumpet sounded a shrill fanfare as we docked.

Beyond the lines of soldiers ashore were gathered a company of more than a dozen finely dressed horsemen. Above their heads floated a standard sporting a scarlet cross on a white background. They dismounted, tossing their horses' reins to a gaggle of waiting attendants, and advanced as the gangplank was thrust out across the last remaining feet of water between ship and dockside.

As Edward prepared to step ashore behind several burly soldiers of his own, Lord Francis said softly, 'Lord Kildare is the foremost, his brother Sir Thomas to his side.'

Edward drew in one long, deep breath at the words, releasing it again slowly. But his face betrayed no emotion as he then strode down the plank, followed by Lord Francis, then Alys in a dazzling new azure gown.

All the men upon the cobbled harbourside knelt at their approach.

The leader, a tall, broad man with a neatly clipped

black beard, unsheathed his sword and held it up, pommel first, towards Edward, before placing it on the ground at his feet.

As I stepped on to the gangplank, eager to reach dry, unshifting land again myself, the man's words reached my ears, carried on a strange, gruff but lilting accent.

'Welcome to Ireland, my liege. I and my men are ready at your command, and my house is yours while you tarry here.'

15

A Dublin Welcome

Gerald FitzGerald, the Earl of Kildare, was a man of his word, as we discovered over the days and weeks to come. Though his apartments in the ancient castle in Dublin had few of the luxuries to which we had become accustomed in Mechelen, it was a relief to be there after the privations and dangers on board ship – and comfortable in its way.

Yet it was the welcome we received from the people that perhaps stood out. Or at least the welcome they gave to Edward, Alys and Lord Francis, in particular. I was assigned at first to the servants' quarters as befit my station as – well, as servant. In Flanders, where Edward's status was still uncertain – nephew to Duchess Margaret, cousin by marriage to Duke Maximilian, but not a ruler in his own right recognized by others in Europe – I could pass as a boyhood companion. But here in Dublin, a strict hierarchy was observed. Already acknowledged king by the FitzGeralds – his deputies in Ireland – Edward was viewed as an adult and only gentlemen were suitable as companions. I was not trained to be his body servant either, and again I was neither one thing nor another – an outsider once more.

Before long Edward was embraced by all the local lords as their king, the latest flowering of the Plantagenet dynasty and the Yorkist hope to which all were devoted after the good governorship of his father, grandfather and uncle. Lord Francis also had their acclaim as loyal friend and counsellor to the late lamented King Richard, whose brief reign had promised so much for this outpost of English rule. And Alys – well, she soon became the favourite of all the ladies, but especially of Lady Kildare. The earl's wife took her under her wing within minutes of our arrival.

'Come with me, my dear.'

This short woman, made plump by signs of a coming happy event, enveloped Alys in her wide-open arms before hurrying her away from the great hall. As they passed me, standing among the still-loitering attendants, her next words just reached my ears.

'We'll soon have you comfortable again after the horrors of your voyage.'

Alys's eyes rolled heavenward as she saw me watching, but she allowed herself to be bustled out the door. And when I next encountered her, some hours later as the household prepared for supper, she did indeed look more rested and happier than at any time since we departed from Sluis.

'Lady Kildare is very kind,' she murmured to me as we rinsed our hands in the basins held by boys at the entrance to the great hall. 'I shall ask her to find you a more suitable lodging, perhaps among the squires if you wish.'

'Don't worry,' I told her. 'I am content where I am.'

In truth, it still rankled that I had never become a squire, despite my efforts at weapons training in London and Flanders, and I had no wish to live among those of my own age who were more fitted for any battles that might come. As we entered the hall, I mulled over whether perhaps it was time simply to accept that my role as scribe, or perhaps secretary, was the best I could hope for. And to be sure, when my thoughts drifted back to King Richard's secretary, Master John Kendall, I knew I could be of use. Master Kendall had served first duke, then king loyally for many years – and despite being a man of words, not of the sword, he had remained with his master up to the very end. Would I ever muster the courage to do the same?

That first evening in Dublin was passed quietly, with a good supper provided for us newcomers and the earl's household only. Edward was honoured with the central seat upon the dais, flanked by the earl and his lady,

Sir Thomas and his young son Maurice, and of course, Lord Francis, Alys and the Burgundians. But messages had been sent out to the great families of the area to assemble the following day for a feast to celebrate the arrival of the new king.

On the morrow, Edward, attired in the finest fashions brought with him from Burgundy, sat in state on the earl's great carved chair, Lord Kildare to one side, Lord Francis and Sir Thomas to the other, while wave after wave of local knights and their grown sons came to do him obeisance. They all remained standing until the final bows had been made, then at a word from the earl, dropped upon their knees, clapped their right hands over their hearts, and raised their voices in an almighty clamour. At first their words were familiar – an oath to serve their king till death – but then some guests continued the acclamation in language I could not even guess at.

A local squire, seeing puzzlement on my face, leaned across to me.

'The words they are saying are from an age-old ceremony,' he whispered in his heavily accented English. 'The high kings of old would be swearing to serve and be served by all the many chieftains of these lands. Their lordships are using the ancient tongue of our people.'

I later learned this was the language of most of the people of Ireland. In Dublin the nobility and greater part of the citizenry now spoke only English, or sometimes Norman French as in the old days. But beyond the robust walls of this city long ruled by the Plantagenets and their lieutenants, the Irish tongue was spoken by peasants and lords alike. I found it a lyrical language, well suited to songs of both a rustic and a more courtly nature.

In the days after the welcome feast, I sought out the musicians who had played that evening and found them willing to teach a foreigner the rudiments of their craft and of their tongue. In their kindness they also passed on some skill with a harp, an elegant stringed instrument much like the lyre of classical tales. It offered a lilting backdrop to the songs I learnt – and also could provide the foundation for many a rousing dance tune. Lutes these musicians also possessed, and they would have spared me one for my use. But the memories stirred were bitter to me, and I preferred now the lightness of the new instrument.

Soon I could join their troupe as they played and sang for the earl, his family and honoured guests as they relaxed in the evenings, though I knew never again would I be called upon as a solo performer. Although pleasant enough, my voice had lost the high beauty and clarity that had bewitched listeners, including my master King Richard, when I was a young boy. Its quality had always been a surprise to me, despite the many hours of training over the years at song school and after. Yet I now missed it less than I would have expected. Those days when I might have sounded like an angel were long past, part of another life I could never reclaim. Now was a time for moving on.

My between-two-worlds status – neither servant only nor true gentleman – was a puzzle to the earl and his household, and in time Alys manoeuvred me into a more settled role by way of her growing friendship with Lady Kildare. I suspect Lord Francis also had a hand in the change, watchful as he ever was of Edward's welfare and changeable moods. Before the grand and boisterous Yuletide festivities were long past, I had been moved into a small antechamber adjoining Edward's own rooms and was accorded more deference by the other serving men. Edward himself hardly noticed the change, but I was well used to his reserved ways by this time.

Indeed, although those first weeks in Dublin passed at a slow pace for Alys and me, Edward had plenty to keep him busy, without the need to observe such minor events. For, since they had received word of the young Plantagenet's claim and imminent arrival in their country, Lord Kildare and Sir Thomas had been labouring hard to win more of the Irish nobility to Edward's cause, not only those who lived or had lands close to the city, in the area known as the Pale. There English kings had always enjoyed their strongest support, since the second King Henry had invaded the country and forced it to accept his overlordship. I soon learned that the greater part of the island of Ireland had barely been brought under the control of the English crown, despite the might of its kings and the centuries Ireland had paid tribute to them. The clans – extended families held together by individual chieftains – still went their own ways and squabbled amongst themselves as they had done long before the coming of the English. To bring them together in peace beneath the rule of any king, let alone a new one fresh from Flanders, would be the work of much skill and effort, and not a little time.

Lord Francis now joined his endeavours to those of the earl and his brother, and over the weeks after our arrival, a string of lords and chieftains, speaking all varieties of English, French and the native Irish tongue, arrived as guests of the Kildares, to be greeted and feasted with no expense spared. Much of Edward's time was spent in meetings with these men and their counsellors, and many were the promises made to him of loyalty and soldiers, and of joining him on his quest to reclaim his throne, before the lords departed back to their ancestral lands.

Alys passed most of her time in the ladies' quarters, as was to be expected. But on fine days, of which there were many that winter – though rain was a frequent visitor, we shivered through none of the snowfalls and few of the frosts we were used to in England – her request to ride was often agreed to. Lady Kildare, although famed herself as an accomplished horsewoman, in her delicate condition could not ride out with her, so Alys was able to choose her own companion. And fortunately, when Edward was in negotiations with the local warriors, her usual choice was almost always free to join her.

Each morning after breaking my fast with the rest of the household in the great hall, I returned to my chamber and awaited either her or Edward's summons.

Only rarely did Edward himself require me at those times, his discussions being often too secret to admit me, or else he needed no scribe to make notes or write letters for him. But Alys would send for me whenever she could. And I would make sure that suitable horses were made ready for us in the earl's well-stocked stables and await her with some impatience.

I had struggled to make any close friends while residing among the servants, with whom I had fewer dealings after my change of room, and although I enjoyed my time with the musicians, our differences in language proved a barrier to true friendship. Alys was now my only real source of companionship, and I valued those rides with her more that I could express. It was especially difficult to put this into words at first, as of course we were always accompanied on the rides by Alys's Burgundian maid, Berthe.

Alys had become used to Berthe's attentions and her company since leaving Flanders, but as I had seen on our voyage, she tolerated rather than befriended her. She declared the maid was more interested in the sailors and then the squires, 'as though hoping she will find a good match among them'. As ever dismissive of girls who wished to marry and settle down, Alys found Berthe's habits coquettish and had no time for them. Yet they proved to be to our advantage. Berthe was no horsewoman. Alys proclaimed she was even worse than Elen, which I felt was harsh – and she was also less uncomplaining. But within a few weeks she had found herself a sweetheart among the grooms, and after a show of riding out with us each day for the eyes of any ladies or gentlemen who might be watching, she would leave us and double back to pass a pleasant day in his company.

Alys and I had no complaints. At last we could talk freely together, ride as far as we wished, stop at our leisure. Sometimes, when I was sure Edward would not need me for any part of the day, I begged bread and cheese or dried meats from the kitchens, and we roamed the whole of the short winter's day in the gentle-rolling, sparsely wooded countryside outside the city walls.

On all our rides, Shadow loped at our horses' heels, on occasion darting ahead in chase of hare or rabbit. At such times, when the hound's feathery tail windmilled with her speed as she sprinted joyously along the track, images of her sister Murrey often sprang into my mind. The two dogs were so alike, despite their differing colours – white and deep red.

A pang of jealousy would spasm within me at the memory. But always I thrust it aside. Murrey was gone. There was no point in dwelling on it. Alys was not to blame. I could not resent that Shadow still lived.

Perhaps Alys guessed some of my pain, though she never spoke of it. But often at these moments, she would spur her horse forward and call, 'Come, Matt! Why should Shadow have all the fun? Race you to —' and force me to forget, as all my focus must be on staying atop my horse as I chased her to whichever landmark she had chosen.

She always won the contest, of course. She had soon persuaded Lady Kildare to allow her the pick of the earl's impressive stables and had selected a slender-boned but well-muscled grey mare for her usual mount.

As ever, I preferred a quieter, good-natured old beast, the trusted mount of Lady Kildare's eldest daughter before her marriage two years earlier. It reminded me strongly of my old pony, Bess, last seen carrying Lord Francis from the battlefield in the guise of a pedlar. When we met again at Gipping, he had assured me she had been well tended by the brothers at Colchester Abbey where he had received sanctuary and recovered from his battle wounds.

Despite its age, my new horse enjoyed being urged again into life, and the three of us – the laughing girl on her spirited grey, the bounding hound, and me on the rejuvenated bay – would reach the ancient oak, or bridge, or crossroads, or way marker, short of breath but happy, any bitter memories fled.

On those days, between our breathless races, we spoke of many things, though seldom now the past. Perhaps we both sensed it was time to let go of our many sadnesses and look forward to what we hoped – trusted – would be a happier future. It was, however, a future that remained uncertain – for both of us.

My path, I knew, lay with Edward, wherever that might take him – and me. It was not clear yet just what was planned by Lords Lovell and Kildare with their young king in negotiations with their new Irish allies. Whether to strengthen and broaden his rule in Ireland, and wait and hope that Tudor would rise to this challenge and come to meet it head on, or, as Duchess Margaret had suggested, whether an invasion of England itself would be attempted.

Alys's way forward was, if anything, perhaps even less sure. In Lady Kildare she had made another powerful friend, who assured her she could have a home with her in Dublin as long as she wished.

'Lady Kildare is all kindness. And she misses her daughter Margaret terribly. I believe that's why she has taken so to me. She says her daughter and I have the same colour hair – though it will be a long time before mine again reaches the length of hers.'

Her hand crept up to tuck in a light red curl that had escaped from the fur-lined hood of her riding cloak and the linen cap within. I had forgotten until then how short her hair must still be since she cropped it to disguise herself as a boy before our first flight from Gipping.

'Margaret was married so young, Lady Kildare says. She was only twelve. And her other daughters have not yet reached an age where she can speak to them as to another woman. It's almost as though she would adopt me in Margaret's place.' She laughed at the idea.

'But her other daughters will soon grow up,' I said.

'I suppose that's true enough. But Lady Kildare laments that all daughters must go to live with their husbands' families once they marry. She says it was the saddest day of her life, Margaret's wedding day, knowing that would happen. She says it would be a fine thing to have a son, and she enjoys the company of her nephew, but —'

'She doesn't plan to marry you to her nephew to keep you here?'

My question was abrupt, even to my own ears.

Alys reined back her horse, a frown touching her face as she glanced across at me. Had the alarm in my mind forced its way into my voice?

'I mean, he's barely ten, if that,' I said quickly, lest she surmise I had some other reason for my concern. 'And he's not interested in books or poetry or music, or any of the things that you love.'

I had seen enough of Sir Thomas's son to be aware his education extended little beyond training for war and the pleasures of the hunt.

Alys snorted her disdain.

'Matthew, don't be daft! Even if she did have such hopes, she knows I am still Dame Grey's ward. And I'm not of age – not for years yet. No priest would marry me to Maurice without permission.'

'Not even the Kildares' chaplain?' I tried to laugh off my misstep. 'Did you notice him nodding off during Mass last Sunday morning, even between the responses? One of the squires said he'd drunk most of his stock of communion wine the night before. Apparently, Lady Kildare had refused to let him attend her birthday celebrations that evening because he'd embarrassed himself at Mass earlier in the day too – so he had nothing else to drink! The squire seemed to think it was nothing unusual.'

'Really? Do you remember that time Sir William did the same? He claimed it was because it was so cold in the vestry that winter's morning …'

We lost ourselves in good memories from our time at Middleham Castle, and I welcomed the change of course. I was afraid Alys would mistake the reason for my worries about young Master FitzGerald. It was not to do with marriage itself. We had only just been thrown together again, were only now finding ourselves able once more to talk as friends without reserve. The thought of losing that renewed friendship so soon was something I had no wish to face. Although I knew we would likely go our separate ways again before long...

That day, as on every other such, Berthe the maid was waiting for us on our return. She greeted us with a wink and a conspiratorial smile, as though she imagined our pleasures from the day had been the same as hers. Alys and I said nothing to set her right. We had no thoughts of any romance – we were friends, as ever, no more – but we knew our knowledge of the maid's own secret dalliance would seal her lips against telling anyone else of her suspicions about us.

Somehow Lord Francis also knew there was nothing between Alys and me other than an old friendship. Once or twice he encountered us by chance as we returned alone from our rides, before the maid met us just outside the city walls. His face at such times was always pensive, but at sight of us it cleared and he greeted us with good cheer. I knew he had his own suspicions, of course – of Edward, not me. Perhaps he vouched for us and our lack of bad intentions, as after a while Berthe was no longer required to ride out with us – to her immense disappointment at having her own little subterfuge ended.

Sometimes Edward escaped from his usual occupations and joined us on our rides, but on other occasions I was requested to remain behind with him.

One such came early on in our stay. Not so early that the pleasures of Yuletide were too distant a memory – with near-constant feasting, the skirl of pipes and thrumming of harps supplying the background to the swirl of ladies' skirts in the dancing, the raucous mumming and rich gifts, all overshadowing the solemnities of the season of Our Lord's nativity. Yet before the days began to lighten or lengthen, or the frosts lessen, or the buds fatten on the blossom trees in Lady Kildare's pleasure garden, an important visitor arrived demanding to meet with Edward.

He came from faraway England. From Henry Tudor himself.

16

Inquisition

I drew myself up as straight and tall as I could.

I was conspicuous, I knew, and uncomfortable. My instinct was to hide myself away. But Edward had insisted I stand ahead of the Kildare squires and the rest of the assembled household. I was the only person here who wore the royal Plantagenet livery – my new tunic of murrey and blue with white rose and sun in splendour – and Edward wanted it to be seen. And for once I had given in to his request that I unpin King Richard's silver boar from the fabric.

He himself wore again his finest armour, kingly surcoat and his father's great sword as he stood waiting on the dais, Lord Kildare and Sir Thomas to one side, Lord Francis to the other. Above them hung the royal standard, still now, but a proud proclamation to any who should approach.

And once we were all in place, and all likewise still – when even the smallest page at the far end of the great hall had ceased his fidgeting – the waited-for visitor did indeed approach.

A sonorous knock, and the huge wooden doors opened to reveal Lord Kildare's herald. Beside him stood a man of above middle age and above middle height, swathed in robes adorned with the cross of St George and other heraldic devices mostly unknown to me. Beyond were arrayed a small company of men similarly attired with the English saint's cross. All stepped forward a pace or two with the herald as he announced,

'Your Grace, my lords, ladies and gentlemen. His lordship, Garter King of Arms, Sir John Wrythe, come from England to speak with His Grace, King Edward, King of England and France, and Lord of Ireland.'

A ripple of whispering spread among the gathered crowd as the Garter King strode past, across the rush-strewn, stone-flagged floor, followed by his gentlemen. It died away as he halted before the small group on the dais, replaced by a tense silence as we waited again. What would be the action of this envoy of the man who now claimed he was King of England?

The newcomer stood for a moment, his hand resting on the hilt of his sword, his gaze resting on the tall silent young man before him. From where I stood to one side, I saw a grizzled head with a lined face, eyes narrowed as though in thought, and lips drawn tight. Then that head was bowed and the man lowered himself to his knee, the tip of the scabbard of his sheathed sword grating along the ground as he did.

The faintest breath of a sigh rose from those gathered behind me, but now I had eyes only for Edward. Lord Francis had insisted he greet Tudor's envoy as true king, in a proper royal audience. Hence the care with which all had dressed and assembled.

Edward did not disappoint. As I had seen him do to his uncle, Duke Richard, at Stony Stratford almost four years ago, and more recently to Master Tournier aboard our ship, he held out his left hand to the Garter King. The cool winter light streaming through the hall's high windows glinted off the huge stone of his ring like sunlight off an ice-bound pool. And, with just the slightest hesitation, the English envoy grasped the hand and drew it to his lips, planting a kiss on the jewel.

Only then did Edward break his silence. His voice now was not piping and boyish as when he had addressed his uncle, but the deeper, assured tone of rightful king. But, close as I was, I could see the emotions fighting within his clear blue eyes.

'We greet you well, Sir John. We trust you have been tended to well after your strenuous journey.'

The Garter King raised his head to reply, but not yet his body. He could not stand until bidden by the king.

'I have been treated well, indeed, since we arrived, I thank you, sir.'

A gasp flew up from a hundred mouths at the words, though they were courteously spoken.

Sir Thomas lunged half a pace towards the still-kneeling man, his fist upraised, but Edward's own hand shot out to stop him. The older man rocked on his heels as a look sped between them, and Edward's fair head shook minutely. Stepping back again, Sir Thomas struggled to quell his anger. His chest rose and fell rapidly and his face was purple with a rage he could not easily wipe away.

Edward's own features were a mask as he released Sir Thomas's fist and turned back to the Garter King.

'I shall overlook your slight, my lord, intended though it may have been. I am fully aware of why you are here and that your master has instructed you in how to act and speak. I fear the Earl of Richmond has had little time to acquaint himself with the niceties of diplomacy since his usurpation of the English crown.'

The Garter King bowed his head again at this as if in assent, a tiny smile tugging at the corner of his mouth. I doubted Edward could see this from where he stood above the man, but I tucked it into my memory to tell him later.

'I beg pardon, my lord. Let me assure you, no slight was intended. My master, my liege lord, King Henry the Seventh of England, has bid me greet you most cordially and extend the hand of friendship to all in this his territory of Ireland, including his governors here.'

His glance flickered towards the Kildares. The earl regarded him coolly and Sir Thomas had by now mastered himself. They both nodded at him, before turning their attention back to Edward.

'And I would thank your master in a fitting way for his words if he were here.'

A titter of hastily suppressed laughter ran around the company at Edward's words, but neither he nor Sir John showed any sign of hearing it, as he continued.

'Instead I charge you to take my response to

Henry Tudor when you return to him in due course. And I trust you will do that most faithfully.'

'Aye, my lord. That I will. As faithfully as mortal man is able.'

'Then rise to your feet, Sir John, and we shall speak in some privacy.'

Edward extended his hand towards the Garter King again, this time to assist him to stand if he should need it.

Lord Francis and Lord Kildare exchanged a glance across Edward's bent back, approval in their faces. Then both men fell in behind their king and his guest as they walked towards the door set into the nearest tapestry-clad wall. Sir Thomas, several men from the envoy's company and a smattering of other gentlemen also joined the small procession.

I had not received instruction on what to do after the reception of the visitor, but as Lord Francis followed Edward and Sir John into the more private chamber beyond, he sought my eye and crooked his finger at me. His other hand mimed a quill scribbling on paper. So I quietly tagged on to the end of the line of gentlemen and was the last into the room before a servant closed the door behind us.

Lord Kildare's private chamber was arranged to receive a very special guest, with many of the best chairs from about the castle's great chambers gathered together in one place rather than the more usual stools. Edward's seat was the closest to the blazing fire in the immense fireplace, with lesser ones set about it, at increasing distance from the flames. Flagons and goblets and platters of sweetmeats were arrayed upon the oak table for the refreshment of all. And in one corner I espied a small desk, with sheets of paper, quills and inkwell upon it, and a stool set ready. There I seated myself to await what should unfold.

Although I did as Lord Francis had indicated as best I could, so much talk, so much laughter, so many raised voices cutting across one another and so much confusion descended on the room – with all those men and all their views and all the wine that was gulped down – that I must have missed noting down nine-tenths of what was discussed. But both he and Edward were pleased with what little I did record when I showed them my efforts later.

Lord Kildare and his brother had joined the three of us in Edward's own chamber after the meeting had finally broken up. By rights we should have been preparing ourselves for supper with the visitors and the ladies of the household, but their lordships had wished to discuss privately with Edward how the day had gone. And to all four, it seemed everything had gone well.

'Did you make a note of what Sir John said, Matthew, and of all the questions he asked Edward?'

'I believe so, my lord. Certainly most of them.'

At the beginning, before the wine had flowed so freely, my task had been easier. I consulted the papers in my hand.

'He began by saying his master had sent him here to discover who exactly Edward is – whether he is who he claims to be. That he was chosen because he had been chief herald for many years, under our late kings. And he proceeded by asking such questions as his name, parents, lineage, date and place of birth, where he spent his early years, the names of his nurses and tutors.'

But, as Sir John had said after Edward had offered his replies,

'Perfectly answered, my lord, but these are simple questions, of course – the answers to all of which could be taught by anyone with knowledge about England and its kings. Now, my lord, I would have you tell me what happened to you in the year of Our Lord 1483 – from the spring when His Grace, King Edward the Fourth departed this life.'

This tale was less simple, of course – as difficult to relate as it would likely be for any young boy who had

144

lived through the grief and tumult and uncertainty of those days. And Edward, although he had spoken of it all again and again – and in particular, in preparation for just such a day as this, if it should come – still found it hard. I watched again the grief and anger and frustration and resentment well up in him as so often before, and prayed that this time he would conquer it all and present the story to the Garter King with as little passion as possible.

He began well enough, with barely a tremor in his voice as he told of his uncle Rivers breaking the news of his father's death to him at Ludlow. But as he reached those days in the Tower of London – those days of treachery and betrayal as he would always view them – his jaw tightened, and it was as though a shutter were lowering across his eyes, darkening the brightness of a lantern. As he started to recount his uncle Richard's visit to him and his younger brother in the royal apartments, his words stuttered to a halt.

The gentlemen about him looked to each other in consternation, Lord Francis especially.

Sir John's eyes narrowed, even while his gruff voice soothed, 'Pray take your time, my lord. These are weighty matters.'

I was upon my feet before I knew it, deserting my task, and at the table pouring ruby wine into an ornate gilt cup. Wending my way between the chairs, with their seated statues hardly breathing as they watched Edward, transfixed. Bowing before him, seeing the paralysis, in his eyes and the set of his jaw, and also the flicker of fear. Setting the goblet and tiny tray of sweetmeats on the table at his side, as I had for his uncle so many times.

'Take a drink, perhaps, Your Grace. You must be parched after so much questioning.'

His eyes sought mine in gratitude, and he clutched the goblet and gulped at it as though indeed he suffered a great thirst. And Lord Kildare picked up on the cue, leaping to his feet and urging all the gentlemen to fill their cups 'while His Grace takes a moment to refresh himself'.

The gentlemen needed no more encouragement after the tensions of the day so far. For several minutes there was much scraping of chair legs on the stone floor, clinking of jugs on goblets, sloshing of liquids, courteous offerings of tasty morsels, and laughing apologies of those getting in each other's way in the crowded chamber.

Lord Francis, no goblet yet in his hand, caught me as I returned to my corner. His hand gripped my arm as he muttered, 'That was well done, Matthew,' before he knelt down beside Edward.

I heard him say in an undertone, 'Take time to compose yourself, Edward. You are doing well. Your uncle would be proud of you, and your father too, I'm sure,' before I moved on back to my stool. I hoped his lordship's mention of King Richard would not do more harm than good.

My fears were unfounded.

Once the cacophony died down and all were seated for the next act of the drama, Edward continued his story with more aplomb and less emotion. He told of the months after his and young Richard's removal from the Tower in the wake of their attempted abduction – the worry during the October rebellion against King Richard, his subsequent parting from his brother when they were kept separately and in secret at various safe strongholds around the country, their ultimate reunion at Sheriff Hutton, and then finally their stay at Gipping once all interest in their whereabouts had died down.

'It was there I last saw my mother, Queen Elizabeth, after she finally left sanctuary at Westminster.'

Edward paused and took another swallow of wine.

My stomach lurched, for I knew the recent silence of his mother often played on his mind.

But I need not have worried.

'What happened then, my lord?' Sir John prompted. 'After the battle at which King Richard was slain.'

And Edward told of our flight to Lowestoft, across

the sea to Friesland and then to Mechelen, calmly and clearly. Far more so than had I been asked to relate it. I noticed he made no reference to his injury, or the part Hugh and Ralph Soulsby or their uncle played in it. Was that deliberate for some reason I could not guess – or did he just believe it didn't matter?

Sir John nodded once or twice during the story of the plans made and gone astray, and glanced my way with little interest as I was mentioned as the servant of the London merchant charged with arranging the escape. He asked the name of the merchant involved.

Edward shook his head.

'I cannot tell you that, sir. Though I believe he has moved his business to the continent, he may still have dealings with merchants in England. I don't wish to jeopardize his trade.'

Sir John laughed for the first time that day – though not the last.

'I perceive you have a commercial mind, my lord. Like your – like King Edward himself. Nay, do not worry about his interests. If I swear to you on my honour that I will not pass his name to my master, will you tell me? It may help your case. I knew a little of King Richard's dealings in the city – and King Edward's before him.'

So he swore and Edward told him what he knew of Master Ashley, and Sir John nodded again, before asking what happened next. And so the tale was told up to the present time, and Edward finally fell silent.

After another pause and more refreshments all round, other questions had come, many and intimate, and about much that I had not known. About Edward's life at court, at Ludlow with his uncle, about festivities he had witnessed, great events seen from within the royal circle. Even about his brother Richard's wedding.

I had had no idea about that – that young Richard had even been married. After all, the boy I'd first met at Gipping even now was only thirteen or so.

'I remember little of the ceremony, sir. I was only

147

seven or so. Richard himself was only four, I believe, and his bride only a little older.'

I stored this information up to share with Alys next time she spoke about marriage at too young an age, though no doubt she already knew of it. As she'd once told me, the royal family had different customs when it came to such matters. To Edward it appeared nothing unusual.

'I understand my father arranged their marriage so her estates and titles would go to my brother and therefore our family. I recall best the magnificent tournament afterwards. My uncle Rivers often reminded me of it in after years as he had a hand in organizing it.'

And he regaled us with the memories of a seven-year-old boy of perhaps his first tourney.

The thundering of horses in the joust and the splintering of lances on burnished armour and painted shields. The deafening blarings of the trumpeters, the shrill whinnies of the destriers, the sickening crashes as they fell in the lists. The clashes and clangings of swords in the hand-to-hand combats. The gasps and cheers of the crowds. The brilliant rainbow of silks and brocades and precious velvets of the gowns and robes, and the sparkling gold and jewels of the prizes presented to the winners by the tiny bride herself.

'Little Anne died, of course,' Edward said, with scant emotion. 'A year or two before my father did. She was just eight, maybe nine. I only met her once or twice, so I hardly knew her. I don't think Richard did really either. He's never talked of her to me.'

All the guests were silent at this, occupied with their own thoughts, or perhaps ghosts from their own pasts. After a moment or two, our host, Lord Kildare, rose again and ordered more wine and sweetmeats be brought. And he invited more questions and comments from his guests. In the ensuing lively discussion among the gentlemen, it became obvious to all there what would be the outcome of the visit.

Now, in Edward's private chamber, my brief recap

ground to a halt in the confusion of what remained of my notes.

Lord Francis, warming himself in front of the fire, nodded at me, then directed his next words to Edward, who sat in the one chair that remained in the room.

'It is well that Sir John craved pardon for his early insult, Your Grace,'

'Indeed,' agreed Lord Kildare. 'I feared my brother here would be striking him for calling you "sir" rather than "Your Grace" – or at the very least "my lord".'

'So too did I,' said Edward, his lips tightening in a wan smile. 'And while I applaud Sir Thomas for his loyalty, it would not have made the day any easier.'

Lord Kildare bowed his agreement, then swung round to me.

'And did our young scribe here record the apology?'

I shuffled through my papers again. 'I believe so, my lord.'

'And when Sir John said he had served both King Edward and King Richard for many years and had no doubt in his mind that our young king here is exactly who he says he is? That the way he looks and speaks and acts, and his perfect French and Latin and knowledge of life at court, must prove this?'

'Aye, sir – word for word.'

'And,' his brother sported a wide grin as he raised his goblet in a salute to Edward, 'did you get the bit when your man Sir John called Tudor a mean part-Welsh part-French upstart with no right to defile the throne of England?'

To that question I had to shake my head. By that stage of the meeting the room had been in uproar and I had given up any hope of continuing my task.

'No matter,' Lord Kildare laughed. 'It was scarce diplomatic of him, after all, and it may be best there is no record of his words.'

Their lordships, Edward included, appeared more

relaxed than since the early days after our arrival, when the work of persuading local lords to Edward's cause had begun in earnest. Lord Francis was still reserved, as so often, despite also partaking of a little of Lord Kildare's good wine, but even he permitted himself to smile at the turn of events.

'All this gives us hope, gentlemen. When Sir John reports back to his master, and word gets out that the Garter King of Arms believes Edward to be the son of old King Edward, then we can expect an increase in support for his claim to retake the English throne.'

'Yet Tudor will not be giving up without a fight.' Sir Thomas's words were more sober now.

'And nor will his Lancastrian supporters. We would not expect that, no matter how many at home or abroad come out for Edward's cause. But the wavering Yorkists – those who remained uncertain of King Richard's right to the throne, despite all the evidence placed before them – they will have no reason now not to declare for Edward.'

As I watched, Edward seemed to sit a little straighter, taller, in his cushioned chair before the fire. Yet at his lordship's next words, a shadow returned to his eyes.

'But we must not forget what else Sir John said. That Tudor seeks to dissemble, to put out false information about Edward. It will likely not now be enough that the Garter King has met him – even if he is able to state publicly that he is Edward of York.'

''Tis true,' declared Lord Kildare. 'They say that at first Tudor put word about that Yorkists were claiming His Grace was his own brother, young Richard. And then, when it became clear that his name is Edward, not Richard, Tudor's proclamations put out that he had changed his tune – that he was then saying instead that he is Edward, Earl of Warwick. They insist that such changes in claimed identity cannot display truthfulness.'

'They say I am Warwick? You mean my poor cousin Ned who is a prisoner in the Tower?' asked

Edward. 'I knew him a little when we were at Sheriff Hutton together, though he is so much younger than I am. Why would Tudor say I claim to be him? Especially when he already has him in prison. And he knows Ned can't inherit the throne because of his father's treason.'

'I'm not sure.' Lord Francis's face was thoughtful. 'But he will have his reasons. And that's what we must be wary of. He and those around him are clever. Over the past two years I have come to realize it was perhaps a mistake King Richard made – not understanding just how clever, and how far their web of deceit ran throughout the country and beyond. We must try to stay one step ahead of them – or they will outrun us easily in this race.'

Lord Kildare nodded in agreement, all mirth now dropped away.

'And I wonder what will be happening at this royal council that Tudor has called for next month.'

For Sir John's final words to us before the gathering broke up were:

'I must report what I have found to my master at a special council meeting he has called on Candlemas. His spies have brought him word of your activities both in Flanders and here. He also expects at that time the arrival of an envoy from his paymaster, the King of France. No doubt then he will decide what his next move will be.'

17

'Dangerous Beasts'

Time passed and we heard no more from England after the Garter King's brief stay. Or rather, Alys and I heard nothing. Officially, at least.

There were rumours, always rumours. But we tried to ignore them. We knew, from long experience, that was for the best. And we were unsure whether the stories were of any consequence, and where they came from we had no idea.

An uprising against Tudor in Cornwall. Nothing more was heard. Stirrings of another rebellion in the English-held islands in the Channel. No further news of that arrived. And then, word that little Edward of Warwick, Tudor's hostage, had died in his prison in the Tower of London. Or had he been murdered on Tudor's orders?

When that grim rumour reached his ears, Edward himself could not help but take notice, and he spoke directly to Lord Francis and his host about it. When he rode out with Alys and me the following day – accompanied as we always were at such times by a company of the earl's best men-at-arms for protection – he told us of their reply.

'Lord Kildare admitted he has few spies in England, but Francis receives letters from friends in many parts of the country. He told me not to worry about my cousin. He has had word that he is well. He believes it is a tale put about to confuse people, perhaps prevent them from rising in Ned's name. After all, I gather it's what Tudor and his followers did before – when I and my brother were in the Tower.'

Alys glanced at me and grimaced. We both remembered it well – and our horror at the notion that anyone could have suspected King Richard of murdering his nephews. Of Tudor, however, we did not doubt that he could take such action. But neither of us voiced our thoughts.

'Then Tudor is still worried that Warwick is a threat to him?' asked Alys. 'That's so strange. With Ned being so young and unable to be king – and also his own prisoner.'

Edward shrugged.

'Francis reckons it may be meant to distract people's attention from me somehow. Though how that can be – with Ned so clearly his prisoner … Perhaps, as Sir John said, we'll know more after the royal council. If we get to hear …'

Even Edward was not always party to discussions between Lord Francis and our hosts. They said they didn't want to concern him with details. But on important matters, he was invariably consulted. He was, after all, king, and though, as he often said, he had little experience of life and plans and decision-making, their lordships encouraged him to gain what experience he could. So, although Alys and I had no warning, it was no surprise to him when Lord Francis and his closest gentlemen were not at their usual places at breakfast one morning a few weeks after the Garter King's visit.

We cornered Edward in his chamber as soon after the meal as we could.

'He has had news from England that he says he must investigate.' His tone was light as he answered our questions, but could I detect an underlying strain? 'He wouldn't tell me what exactly, or even who it came from. Just that he had to go.'

'Is it about little Warwick?' asked Alys.

'No – well, yes, perhaps. He's alive. He could tell me that.' He hesitated, then, 'Something happened at or after the royal council, but the reports are all confused. So, he said he must go to find out for himself.'

'But he wouldn't tell you what?' I said.

'He wouldn't – or couldn't, perhaps. But he did say I must continue to hope for good tidings. And that he may be away some time. He may also have to return to Flanders.'

I shivered, though there was, as always for Edward, a welcoming blaze in the chamber's grate. The idea of undertaking that voyage again was a torment – or even the shorter crossing over the northern sea in this winter weather.

I was grateful Lord Francis had not taken Edward with him, as then I would have been obliged to go too. Our life here in Dublin might be unexciting, and often frustrating, but I had no wish at that moment to make any alteration. I knew change would come eventually, but for now, days spent in Alys's company, or learning new music and a new language, or even simply standing ready to serve Edward at his whim, were preferable to travelling over rough seas or rough terrain, sleeping who knew where and encountering who knew what enemies, always uncertain whom one could trust or when or where one's next meal would be. Lord Francis had told me enough about his year and more on the run throughout England for me to be glad I had not been required to join him now.

And he was away for some time as he had warned Edward. Weeks passed with almost no news of him, either good or ill. Letters and messengers arrived for him, which Edward and Lord Kildare opened or spoke with, and then other communications came addressed to the earl from supporters in England. But few of them had word of Lord Francis himself. Even when a group of Cornish gentlemen arrived at the castle – some of those who had been rumoured to be stirring trouble in that region of England – they had no firm information about his lordship.

'Something's been going on in London,' said their leader, a grey-haired old knight called Henry Bodrugan, as he hacked at a joint of beef at supper on the evening of their arrival. 'And we heard rumours of Lord Lovell making mischief up in East Anglia or York or thereabouts.

But news travels hard down our way – and we had some business of our own to deal with.'

As the Kildares laughed along with him and his men, I recalled that Cornwall was about as far from the capital as was Middleham, and at the castle, it could take a week or more to glean news of important events happening in the south. Even with the post-horse system put in place by King Richard during the Scottish wars when he was still duke, it took several days for the riders to carry news to or from old King Edward along the Great North Road. Did they even have such a system linking London and the west country?

Over the following weeks, Bodrugan and his men were followed across the Celtic Sea by more and more men fleeing Tudor. Among them was the former captain of Jersey, Master Harliston. I remembered Lord Francis's interest when Guillaume Tournier mentioned his name on our voyage through the Channel. Had he whipped up those disturbances we'd heard of in the islands?

Yet few of the new arrivals could tell us much more about what was happening in England. Each had had his own 'business' to attend to before being forced to leave home, but each had travelled to Dublin with whatever men he could bring because of one or another rumour. Always rumours. Each of which conflicted with the others, until Alys, Edward and I almost gave up trying to decipher just what was going on in our homeland. But each man who came to the castle to offer his services came because he had heard something.

Perhaps that 'other Yorkists are flocking here …'

'A son of old King Edward is going to rise against the usurper …'

'Lord Lovell is gathering men …'

'The dowager Duchess of Burgundy (or, maybe, Duke Maximilian) is raising troops against England …'

'The young Earl of Warwick is no longer a prisoner and is seeking an army …', or

'Young Warwick's been murdered by Tudor and

must be avenged …'

Few indeed expected to be greeted in the great hall of Dublin Castle by Edward Plantagenet, former Prince of Wales, uncrowned, unanointed King of England, once believed to be dead himself – either by murder or by shipwreck or …

I soon learned that rumours are not just dangerous beasts, but also slippery creatures, that change their shape in each telling, and rarely remain recognizable from one week to the next.

We understood now the truth of Lord Francis's words – that Tudor and his advisers were clever and sought to confuse their enemies. These men who came to Dublin were die-hard Yorkists, mostly men who had never accepted Tudor and had sought to make trouble for him ever since he'd won his crown. They would rally to the cause no matter who was its figurehead. Yet the ordinary people? The country gentlemen who preferred a quiet life? The townsfolk who valued their trade and their privileges? Would they seek vengeance for a disinherited Yorkist prince? Would they welcome a call to arms by a foreign power – or fight against it? Would they even care if they learned that a boy king they thought had died had come back to reclaim his inheritance? Even if they ever heard of that returned boy and his claim …

'What happened at the royal council when Sir John Wrythe told them that I am Edward of York?' was the question Edward asked of all who came. It was the question we all wanted answered after the Garter King's predictions.

But no one answer was forthcoming. Each man said what he could, but often that was little or nothing.

'A royal council was called? I had not heard.'

'Aye, it was to be at Sheen Palace, I believe. Though I heard no report from it.'

'Sir John Wrythe? I thought him long dead. Was he here then?'

'An examination by the Garter King of Arms? No,

I didn't hear tell of that.'

'All we heard was some story of an organ-maker's son and a priest.'

'Or was it a baker's son? From Oxford, I think they said.'

'The priest – Symons or Simmonds – or some such name. And a boy. Claimed to be Richard of York – your brother, of course, Your Grace. Was he ever in Oxford? Is he here now? That's what they're saying in London.'

'Nay, my brother is abroad, safe,' Edward would say, patiently, when this claim came up. 'Are you sure that's what Tudor says?'

'No, no,' some new arrival would chide his companion. 'It's not Richard the boy is claiming to be. It's Edward. Edward of Warwick. Old Clarence's son.'

'But it can't be him, he's in the Tower,' would come the response. 'Isn't he? Or was. Why would he claim that?'

And once more the conversation would go round in circles until our heads spun, and always we were no wiser – could no more grasp what was happening in England, and what Tudor was about, than we could before these men's arrival.

In truth, although I never said it to Edward, I was reminded of those days in London after my return from Bruges in the summer when Duke Richard became king. When one rumour after another swirled among the streets and alleys, each wilder and more fantastic than the last. But then, at least, I had been closer to the centre of events, and to where proclamations were made, and my master, Master Ashley, could seek out people who knew and make certain of the truth – or otherwise – of information that had come to our attention. Here we were so far away, reliant on stories told by people who themselves had been far away from the capital. How were we ever to know for sure what, if anything, was true?

18

A Cuckoo's Call

Spring was well advanced before we were to learn anything more concrete.

Scores or even hundreds of Englishmen had arrived in Ireland with their half-, no, barely even quarter-tales and snippets of information or misinformation, and Dublin city was more bustling than we had ever known it. To be sure, it was also the time of spring fairs and ever-busying markets, with Lent and Eastertide now past, and farmers and market gardeners were flooding in from the surrounding areas to sell their new butter and cheese and eggs, spring vegetables, the first fruits of the year, the last of their stored provisions, smoked and salted meats and fish. Which was just as well, we overheard Sir Thomas say to his brother one hectic suppertime, with all these extra mouths to feed.

Despite all our worries about Lord Francis and the situation in England, it was a delight to wander the streets of the city and watch it come alive after the drabness of the winter, listening to the mixture of languages, watching the loading and unloading of ships out on Wood Quay, breathing in the fresh scents of spring flowers brought in for sale along with farmers' produce. But best of all, as always, was to slip away from the bustle of the city altogether, and Alys and I made sure we made our escape as often as we could.

One fine morning, we set off early. Edward had told me straight after breakfast he would not need me that day. A greater air of melancholy hung about him than had for some time, but he sent me away with few words when I suggested I could stay to help divert him or that he ride out with us instead.

It was well not to persist when he was in such a

mood, as I had long ago learned. So I left him to his own company and soon, Alys and I, with Shadow at our heels, had ridden through the castle's twin-towered gateway, down the steep hill, past squat grey Christ Church Cathedral, and were turning on to the wider thoroughfare of Cook Street, making for the main west gate out of the city.

The street was thronged with goodwives and traders, haggling at the shops and stalls, shaded beneath the buildings' timber overhangs. Their cheerful chatter – a blend of English and Irish – drifted up to us as we rode by, but then behind us changed to angry grumbles, as a clatter of hooves cantering upon the cobbles burst around the corner. It would be upon us in an instant.

We hauled our horses over to the side, close upon the store fronts and now-cowering people, to let the speeding rider pass. But as we did, we discovered, not some urgent messenger charged with delivering a vital missive out in the countryside, but,

'Edward!'

His horse skittered to a halt beside us, tossing its head as though protesting at its treatment. The buyers and sellers about us also made their grievances clear, but seeing the rider's rich clothes and the fine-wrought sword in its jewelled scabbard at his side, were careful to voice them only in Irish. Edward paid little heed, having no knowledge of the language, and before long all the townsfolk had returned to conducting their business.

'Edward, what's wrong? Why are you here – and in such a rush?'

Alys reached out a gloved hand to touch his arm. I had told her of his mood that morning and as ever she was mindful of his welfare.

I cast a glance behind him, seeking the troop of riders that should be there. There was no one, just locals who had now closed in across his wake.

'Where are your guard?' I asked, but somehow knew the answer before he spoke.

'I have not brought them. I came on the spur of the moment. I've told no one. There was no time if I wanted to catch you up.'

'But, Edward —' Alys cast a look about us.

All was peaceful, the shoppers no longer even eyeing us now. But we all knew …

'What if there's trouble? You know Lord Kildare believes Tudor has spies here. What if —?'

'We shall deal with it. You and I and Matthew. He and I have our swords.' Indeed we did, Lord Francis having presented me with a weapon of my own in Mechelen, to thank me for caring so long for his. 'And you – you have a fast horse, and can ride to summon help if need be.'

Alys laughed with him, and even I smiled at his exuberance. But that his melancholy had been replaced by this apparent recklessness concerned me.

Alys, however, showed no such worry. She leaned across and grasped his arm again.

'I'm glad you are come with us. Matt and I have decided to explore the great headland that overlooks the city. We don't know what we shall find, so it will be good to have an extra sword. Just in case.'

A sing-song quality touched her voice now, reminding me of when she and Roger had played at romances long ago. Edward picked up on it, his tone and words echoing hers, as he bowed low from the waist.

'Then we must push on with no more delay, my lady. We have a long ride ahead. Have we provisions for our journey?'

I nodded, pointing to my saddlebags. I was not sure I had enough for three, but I supposed we could eke it out. Alys ate little enough anyway, though what she had was always shared with Shadow.

We urged the horses on, beneath the stout stone gateway, and soon were clopping across the ancient timber bridge spanning the river towards the tangle of suburbs on its northern bank. In minutes the low stone and wooden houses with their long garden plots gave way to farmland and pasturage, and then to rough heathland dotted with scrubby copses of trees. Above us clouds were gathering in the once perfect blue sky, but the morning sun was warm upon our faces, with only the light breath of a rising breeze as we rode up the first slopes of the headland.

This was the first time we had aimed to ride so far out from the city, and our first excursion to the higher ground overlooking the wide river valley. Gradually the city was revealed below us as on an intricate chart, where we could just pick out the squat round towers and gateways of the castle and the sky-mirroring thread of the river. The sea stretched out dark blue-green towards the eastern horizon, fringed now with plumping bolsters of white clouds, tinged grey. We paused for a while in the shade of a stand of hazel, dismounting to rest the horses, and marvelled at the view.

'You almost feel you could see all the way to England,' breathed Edward, entranced.

'And what would we see if we could?' I muttered.

He did not hear, but Alys shot me one of her looks anyway, with an added shake of her head. Maybe she feared my words risked a return of his melancholy. I resolved to be careful what I said after that, as we pushed on towards the top of the headland.

We took our time, picking our way along a path that wound slowly, steadily upwards, rather than heading straight up the steeper slopes. Perhaps it was a sheep track. The grass was cropped short as though by flocks, though no sign of the animals was to be seen. Birds there were aplenty. Skylarks soared high above, almost beyond our sight among the clouds, their melody tumbling down upon our upturned faces. Gulls wheeled, screaming, around the shoreline far below. Dark grey crows with black hoods upon their polls perched gloomily on new-budding branches like waiting executioners. Even early swallows swooped, chasing insects across the green.

And then, almost out of nowhere, came a 'cuck-oo, cuck-oo, cuck-oo' from a tangle of birch and hawthorn a little way ahead.

Alys reined back her grey.

'It's a long time since I heard a cuckoo. Probably not since ... not since our last spring at Middleham.'

'I was never there in spring,' said Edward. His face and voice didn't share the wistfulness of Alys's words. 'Only in winter – the winter after my father died. It is a stark, bleak place.'

'The dale? Never!' Alys leapt to the defence of the place she had called home for so many years. 'You simply didn't see it at its best. When the bright green fronds of bracken were unfolding on the moors amid the gold of last autumn. Or the soft froth of pink-white hawthorn blossom lined the lanes.'

'Or the purple blaze of heather on the hill tops in high summer,' I joined in, adding, 'I was never there properly in the spring either, but it is beautiful. And the castle magnificent.'

Edward eyed us both.

'You sound as though you really love the place. And miss it.' His tone was thoughtful. 'My father told me how much my uncle Richard liked it there, more perhaps than royal houses elsewhere. He used to laughingly call it the Windsor of the north.'

'And understandably so,' responded Alys. 'I have known both places. Middleham may not be as grand or luxurious as Windsor, but it was our home and every bit as comfortable. And we always received a good welcome – and could always trust those about us there.'

Edward gazed back across the wide vista of the sea, spread out before us, greying now under the gathering clouds.

'I too was fond of Ludlow when I lived there. They were happy times. But returning to Windsor – or Westminster – always felt like coming home.'

'That's because your family were there, your real family – your mother, father, brothers and sisters, not just your uncle. It's the people who make a real home, not just a place.'

Alys – orphaned at seven years old. King Richard and Queen Anne, their little son Ed, were the family she had known best.

It was my turn to reach out a hand to pat her arm. For once she did not shake it off.

Did Edward see? Was that why he said to me, a tight smile upon his lips,

'And you, Matt – do you too long to be back at your real home?'

I was not quick enough to place a mask upon my face. But what he saw there, as I withdrew my hand from Alys's arm, made him say swiftly, 'I'm sorry, Matthew. I should not have asked. I suppose it's been a long time for you too – and as difficult, in a way.'

Cuck-oo, cuck-oo cuck-oo.

The calls broke upon us again.

Alys wheeled her mount about towards the sound.

'I think it's over there – in those trees,' she said, pointing forty or fifty yards to our left. 'Do you think we'll be able to spot it?'

'They're supposed to be shy birds,' said Edward, also looking steadfastly away from me. 'But we can but try.'

'Perhaps we can see it stealing the other bird's nest to lay its egg in.'

'Nay,' said Edward, spurring his horse towards the trees where the caller was concealed. 'My tutor said they only call like that when seeking a mate. There will be no egg laying just yet.'

As the three of us rode up to the stand of birch, a confusion of fluttering rustled the new leaves in the heights of the trees, and we caught just a glimpse of a sizeable, drab brown bird as it flew off, its long tail fanned behind it. A moment or two later – cuck-oo, cuck-oo cuck-oo sounded again, a little distant this time, screened by the trunks and scrubby undergrowth before us.

We guided our horses round the copse and up the grassy slope towards the next group of trees, as the monotonous call rang out once more. Try as we might, we could not spy the bird perched among the peeling silver-white bark of those trees' branches or the unfurling green at their tips.

Then – cuck-oo, cuck-oo cuck-oo.

Fainter now.

It had fled further on, up the headland, in its desperate search for an answering call that did not come.

Edward led us, his horse trotting now despite the steepening slope and the roughening rocky ground. The short turf between the stones echoed hollow beneath our horses' hooves, and we had to wind between dense mounds of small-leaved, yellow-flowered shrubs. At one, Edward reined his horse back, pausing our chase.

'Planta genista,' he said, leaning down to break off a sprig. He threaded the golden bloom on to his horse's headpiece, where it shone bright against the dark mane. 'The lowly broom. The plant my forefathers named our family after …'

Then the cuckoo's cry rang out from a clump of trees and bushes on the stony shelf just above us. Once again, a flitter of brown wings and it was off.

Edward laughed.

'He may not yet have attracted a mate, but he has found three willing followers. Or four.' His gloved finger pointed at Shadow, nosing eagerly among the rocky outcrops about us before dashing off ahead, the way the cuckoo had flown.

We followed again, more slowly this time, as the track became still steeper, stones crunching and skittering underfoot. Craggy boulders rose to either side, hemming our way so we could not turn our path aside. Up ahead the grey, rocky almost-canyon reached up to meet the grey lowering clouds, almost fog now, and the far-off crashing of waves drifted up to my ears. Were we nearing the very summit of the headland?

'Take care, Edward,' I called. 'How do we know there are no cliffs ahead?'

He glanced back, ready with another laugh, recalling to my mind his recklessness in the city that morning.

'Do not worry so much, Matt. I shall be careful. I'm sure there's no danger here. Come on, Alys. Let's race to —' and he raised his heels to rake his spurs across his horse's flanks.

I watched what happened next as though time had slowed down. Yet, for all that, I was unable to force myself forwards, towards Edward, to prevent the mishap when it came …

19

'Is She a Witch, Think You?'

As I hesitated, Shadow's lithe white body came hurtling back towards us down the track. At her short, sharp warning bark, Alys tugged back on her horse's reins, puzzlement dashed across her face. But Edward's spurs had done their work and, as he tried to halt his horse, it bucked against his rein, then tried to leap up the path.

Something sprang towards it from the rocks to our right – something swathed all in dark rags, darting towards Edward, hands clawing at his high leather boot in its stirrup.

His horse now rearing up, kicking out at what it couldn't see.

Then Edward – Edward, unbalanced, pitched backwards, falling.

Flailing his arm, but catching only air.

Plunging the great height from the saddle to crash on to the track. The air forced from his lungs as he struck the earth with a great 'flumph' that echoed all along the narrow passage.

Alys screamed 'Edward!' and I was down from my horse in a flash, stumbling towards him and grabbing at the tattered figure before it could flee.

It squirmed and writhed beneath my touch, moaning wordlessly, then screeching a high-pitched shriek. But I held on, despite its threshing limbs and the battering of my ears, and, finally, it fell still and silent in my grip. Shadow leapt around, no longer barking, but darting and dodging about us as though to make sure my prisoner was secure.

Alys had caught the rein of Edward's horse before it could bolt and was staring down at where he lay on the ground, her eyes wide with shock.

He was motionless, crumpled upon his back where he had landed.

But then, as I thrust myself forward, dragging my captive with me, he moved first one hand, then the other, to clutch at his head, and a deep groan escaped from him. A moment or two later, he had pushed himself gingerly up to sitting and was running his hands across his shoulders and flexing each arm in turn. After brushing grit and dust from his brocaded doublet, he seized hold of a nearby rock outcrop to help haul himself up.

Once upon his feet, he dusted himself down again, then swivelled towards me. My captive cringed away and began to wail and snivel again. This time I could make out words – in a woman's voice, cracked, though deep. They were an odd mixture of Irish and English, and I translated for the others as best I could.

'She says she didn't mean to – didn't mean to hurt him or make him fall. She just wanted to stop him.'

Edward paused in his advance, distaste scrawled across his face.

Alys called Shadow to her, and leant down as far as she could from her saddle to stroke the dog's head. Its white hair was bristling up between pricked, alert ears and all along its lean back.

And I looked down and saw for the first time properly what, or who, I held so tight in my grasp.

It was a woman, but one who could barely be recognized as such. Indeed she resembled more a wild animal than anything human.

Shorter than me by some way, she could have been any age above fifty or sixty. The cobweb lines on her face were filled with dirt and grime, black against leathery sun- and wind-burnt skin, and her greasy locks, of dingy white streaked with iron grey, trailed long past her waist.

Now she was still I could feel how thin she was. The bones of the wrists I gripped almost cut through her skin. Her tattered clothes, besmirched with filth and grit, rasped my fingers and I saw they were made of rough

167

hessian, reminding me of a nun's habit. A length of thick rope cinched the rags at her waist, and another loop of cord encircled her neck, as though it were a noose. Her feet were bare, the nails upon them torn and encrusted with mud, and the stench of her unwashed body rising to my nostrils all but overpowered me. When her mouth opened to choke out jumbled words once more, stumps of blackened and rotting teeth were revealed. I turned my head away to dodge the waft of breath that was hotter and more foetid than a hound's.

Edward stood still where he had halted, horror growing on his face.

'Is she a witch, think you?'

I swallowed, trying not to breathe through my nose.

'No, no, I don't believe so.'

Had I seen a glint of madness in her eye as she gabbled at me, just as I now caught the glint of fear in his? I felt the gnarled hands, the bony fingers, clutch at me.

'I'm sure she's harmless – just some poor soul who's lost her way, maybe been cast out of her village.'

Alys nudged her horse closer, gazing down.

'Harmless, you think?' She forced out a half-laugh. 'Some sort of wise woman, perhaps?'

At that the woman spat on the ground at her horse's feet. Alys swung its head around to move away again, as the cracked voice said, in clear but accented English, 'Let me be, let me be. It's not you, it's him I seek.'

My stomach rolled over at the thought she meant me. But now she was staring straight at Edward, who was rooted where he stood, just feet away.

She wrested one hand away from mine and jabbed a bent finger at him.

'It's him, him I seek – the king.'

All colour fled from Edward's face.

Did my features mirror his? I felt as though the woman's cold fingers were clamped about my heart too.

But she made no other move towards him, or away from me. And it was Edward who recovered himself first.

'Why do you seek me, madam?' he asked, his voice tense but calm. 'What do you want of me?'

Alys flung out a hand towards him, beseeching, 'Edward, no!'

But he said again, 'What do you want of me?' and stepped a pace towards the woman.

'Let me go, let me be,' she wheedled once more, shaking herself now against my grip.

I tightened my grasp on her wrist and clutched her rope belt with my other hand. But Edward shook his head. He was staring at her as though under a spell.

'Let her go, Matt.'

I hesitated.

'Let her go.'

He was my king, after all.

I released her wrist, let go of the rope. Stepped after her, close, ready to grab her as she stepped towards him.

But she only took his hand, the one with the great ring upon it, and said, 'Come with me.' And drew him with her as she clambered up over the boulders to the right of the track.

Alys's eyes met mine. She shrugged, helpless, then dismounted and led both horses to scramble up the rocks after them. I brought up the rear, also on foot, the rein of my own mount loose in one hand, while I used the other to steady myself as I picked my way up and over the bank.

As I reached the top, I discovered the reason for the huge fright we had all just suffered.

Barely a score of paces ahead, the rocky grassland fell away in front of us. All that could be seen was a low jumble of rocks, then a roiling mass of cloud and sea fog. Seabirds were screaming and swooping and disappearing down beyond the very end of the land.

Alys and Edward were standing there in silence,

staring. Their horses were fidgeting uneasily, and one of Alys's hands was tight about both their reins, while the other absently stroked the nose of her grey.

Was she, like me, imagining just what would have happened had Edward not been so violently waylaid, and had instead raced recklessly after Shadow and headlong on to this cliff edge?

20

'King that Once Was …'

The woman set off again, still leading Edward by the hand.

A cruel wind had sprung up while we had been sheltered among the trees and rocks and stony canyon, the wind that had swept the bank of fog towards the land so quickly. Now it tore at my hair and face, drying and stinging my lips. As I moistened them with my tongue, I tasted the salt it carried from the sea far below. Above us the billowing blanket of dark grey cloud weighed heavy.

With Alys, I too followed where the woman led, up a gently rising expanse of scrubby heathland. Few trees dotted this slope, lone hawthorns only, no leaves or may blossom yet glimmering upon them. Only their crazed black skeletons emerged from the swirling mist, their limbs reaching ever inland, bent by the wind from the sea. No friendly 'cuck-oo' was to be heard now from among those branches, only the buffeting of that wind pushing us away from the cliff.

'We must be careful, Matthew.' Alys spoke loud enough for my hearing above the wuthering of the wind, but not so loud that Edward or his guide should catch her words. 'It will not be easy to find our way back if this fog remains, and darkness will come on early too.'

I feared she was right. My stomach told me it was not long past noon, but it would be difficult to tell of time passing with no sun to be seen. And our encounter with this strange woman had lent an odd, magical quality to the day that might mislead us yet more.

'Let us see where she leads us, then we can take stock. I doubt Edward in this mood will welcome us interfering now. And she seems to mean him no harm.'

Edward had spoken not a word – to us or the woman – nor looked back at us since she had taken his hand, and was letting himself be shepherded who knew where. If I believed in sorcery, I might almost have said he appeared bewitched. Had I been too quick to dismiss his question before? But as Alys had hinted, people thought to be such were often simply wise women, if a little strange in their ways or different in their heads.

She nodded her own head now.

'Agreed. But we must be watchful.'

The woman led us on, always upward towards the mist, with the sea far below us to our left. The fog and cloud had closed in to less than a hundred paces now, and I could no longer spy the land's end. I was glad to move further away from that precipitous edge, and I knew also that every step this way took us closer to the city – though I had no notion what terrain lay between us and there. From time to time the fog lessened – or was it a gap splitting the clouds? – and the distant hollow booming of waves drifted up to us, carried on the still-freshening breeze. Memories of the storms of our late voyage flooded back, and I hoped few sailors were out there on the Celtic Sea today.

The ground under our feet flattened out, and in the mist ahead, grey formless shadows loomed. As we walked on, they merged into shapes of rocks, and fallen slabs, then half-raised stone walls. Or, as we drew nearer, more like half-ruined. One sloped up from waist height and stretched seawards away from us, then heaved itself up into a bulk far above our heads topped by a well-carved arch. Within the arch, stone tracery cut broken circles stark against the dark clouds, and it struck me where we were.

'A chapel of some kind,' I breathed. 'But … up here?'

'I've heard Lady Kildare say that in ancient times, monks in Ireland built their abodes all over the wild places,' Alys said, her voice touched by awe. 'They sought peace in the wilderness away from townsfolk. Maybe this is one such.'

Edward and the woman paid us no heed, making

their way along the wall until they found a doorway. Only half a stone upright remained, a deep, narrow hole bored into it, and a hollowed slab as a threshold, worn away perhaps by centuries of passing feet. The building's floor, which in our churches might have been stone flags or even beautiful tiles with symbols of Christ or his saints, was only grass and the pink flowers of sea thrift nodding in the wind.

Two more broken-down walls completed the chapel, and the woman led Edward – and us – to where one met the high, arched wall of the east end. In the corner was a rough shelter – a roof of thin branches and reeds supported on what may have been ancient roof timbers. Piled-up animal skins lay within, and just outside, blackened stones edged a small hearth, enclosing ashes and burnt twigs like charcoal.

'She lives here?' The words forced themselves past my lips.

The woman glanced my way, then dropped Edward's hand at last and ducked into the hovel. She emerged bearing a rough clay jug and cup and, placing the latter in his hands, poured water into it.

'Drink, lord,' she insisted, in English.

He did as he was bid, his movements still slow and dreamlike. As I watched, I recollected the contents of my saddlebags. In a moment I had brought forth our leathern water bottles and cloth-wrapped packages of wheaten bread, salt beef, soft creamy cheese, and half a dozen small hard wrinkled apples that had survived storage over winter. A slab of stone to one side had clearly been swept clean of moss and lichen, and on this I spread our bounty.

Alys, seeing what I intended, waved her hand at it and invited, 'Share with us and eat, madam.'

A frown crossed the woman's lined face, but then it cleared and a smile of sorts revealed her rotten teeth.

'Our Lord broke bread and ate his Last Supper for us,' she said, again in her mix of Irish and English, and I realized what I had done. Propped against the wall just behind the cleared slab was a rust-encrusted crucifix, traces of gilt shining bright here and there about tiny hollows with broken metal claws that once perhaps held minute gems. The flat stone was her altar.

But she was unbothered.

'Eat,' she said, this time in English, and herself took a small portion of bread and set to.

It was perhaps the strangest meal I ever ate, perched there on the grassy ground in the old, ruined chapel, well sheltered from the wind. I watched the delicate way both Alys and the old woman ate, but all the time my stomach was grateful I had brought more food than I had supposed. Shadow alone missed out. She lay stretched out at Alys's feet, her brown eyes gazing up, full of resentment. Alys ruffled the fur on her head, but did not give in. Later she told me she could not feed a hound when this woman clearly had so little.

The woman herself ate just a little bread and cheese and a single apple with obvious relish, but left the meat to us. Maybe, as her ragged clothes might suggest, she had once been in a religious order, and one that ate no meat, even on non-fast days.

Our meal done, I tidied away the wrappings into my saddlebags. As I turned back, the woman seized Edward's hand again, tugged him to his feet and pulled him over to the cross. He had said not a word since we arrived at this strange place and now did her bidding again without question.

She bent down and, grasping the iron crucifix with both hands, offered it to him. Somehow, without her speaking, he knew what she wanted of him, and he pressed his lips to the rusty object to kiss it. She nodded and muttered a few words of Latin I couldn't catch, then with both hands raised the cross above her head.

To my surprise, while we had been sitting there, the darkest clouds had blown away and the sky was now a mosaic of broken blue and high white billowing clouds. A single shaft of sunlight slanted through the high window tracery and glinted off a shred of gilding on the cross.

The woman spoke again, louder now but to Edward alone, reverting to her blend of languages and repeating her words over and over while I translated.

'Pray to the Lord, Edward, son of Edward, son of Richard – king that once was, king that shall be.'

Alys clenched my arm as I spoke the words a second time, the speaker nodding now at me. Her fingers pinched and her eyes were once more wide with alarm.

'Matt, we must go,' she hissed. 'We must get him away from here.'

But the old woman had snatched at Edward's wrist again to keep him close, and he showed no sign of wanting to leave. He only gazed down into her face, his eyes brimming with questions, and her eyes held his. Her words now were slower, more deliberate, more in English than Irish.

'I remember your grandfather, Richard of York. A fine man, Ireland's friend. He should have been its king. But he left, went far away, over the sea. He never came back, and was king of nowhere. Do not make his mistake. Do not go over the sea. You may never come back – you too may be king of nowhere.'

Alys lunged forward and tore the woman's hand away from Edward, ripping the crucifix from her other hand and thrusting it back on the altar slab. She clasped Edward's shoulders and twisted him to face her.

He winced at her touch and his face was all confusion. But he stared at her as though he was a parched man beholding shimmering spring water.

'Edward, we have to go – now. This – this mad woman cannot help you.'

The woman clawed at them both with her fingers outspread, but Alys shoved her away with an outstretched arm, not even looking at her. I grabbed her, this time by her rope belt, and swung her without difficulty towards her shelter, marvelling that she weighed little more than Shadow, who was now prancing about her, barking. The woman made no resistance, no move towards Edward, but stood there, simply staring now, silent.

Alys dragged the stupefied Edward to his horse.

'Mount,' she ordered, and watched while he did, before gathering her own reins and gesturing to me to help her. In a few seconds all three of us were upon our horses, and Alys was steering our way out of the ancient ruin. As my horse stepped over the worn stone threshold, I glanced back at the old woman. She was standing still by her shelter, having made no further movement, but now she raised her voice again.

'Beware your enemies. Beware also your friends.'

Alys guided Edward's horse as though he were an infant learning to ride and did not stop until the ruin was out of sight, hidden behind a series of hillocks edging the pathway on the seaward side. Then she pulled her horse and Edward's to a halt and turned to him.

'Are you all right?'

'Yes. No. I don't know. I think so.' He shook his head as though driving away sleep. 'She spoke of my father – and of my grandfather. Do you think she knew him?'

'Your grandfather? I don't know. Perhaps. But it doesn't matter. She's just a cracked old woman.'

'But my grandfather. She said he should have been king – but never was.'

'Everyone knows the story of your grandfather,' I put in. 'That he should have been king. Would have been – if it hadn't been for the Lancastrian usurper Henry the Fourth – or his son and grandson.'

'Matt's right,' said Alys. 'Everyone knows that. And that he was governor of Ireland before he went home to England to claim his throne. It doesn't mean she knew him. Or that he shouldn't have tried.'

At those words, of a sudden I understood her violence in the chapel. She was worried Edward's doubts would resurface. It was not just the eeriness of the situation, the mad woman's strange words – but the effect they might have. And I recalled her words to me in Mechelen about the need to encourage him.

'But never mind that,' she continued, casting a glance backward. 'We should get away from here and back to the castle as soon as we can. The weather may close in again. We don't want to miss our way.'

From where we were now, the sea was visible again, and though the sky was only patchy with cloud, fog clustered still about the shoreline below. Trails even snaked along the course of the great river, up as far as and beyond the deep Pool at the east of the city where only the largest sea-going ships docked – where we had sailed in on our arrival all those weeks ago, with Edward's royal banner streaming proud above us.

As I squinted down towards the river, the curtain of mist about the entrance to the Pool parted for a few moments, revealing three huge ships making their stately way into its harbour. I had spent much time at the Pool during our time in Dublin, as I had in the main city docks of Wood and Merchants' Quay, watching the unloading of exotic goods from all over the continent and chatting to sailors of many lands when their work was over for the day. Yet I had never seen more than one ocean-going ship there at a time, often not even that. Most shipping could now sail upriver into the heart of the city since the quays had been built many years before. Three ships would be quite a sight to behold.

As I pointed out the ships to Edward and Alys – neither of whom, it must be said, had as much interest in merchants' dealings and adventures as did I – an orange flash burst upon the round watchtower at the Pool's entrance, and a split second later a ringing blast struck our ears.

My breath caught at my throat. Though so distant, and so much quieter than I had known before, there was no mistaking the sound – one I had not heard since a fateful day almost two years before.

'What's the matter, Matthew?' Alys's voice was

177

full of concern

'That was the retort of a cannon. I heard them in the battle, though closer to. Is the city being attacked?'

Edward only laughed.

'I think not.' The sight of the ships and firing of the cannon – and perhaps my ignorance – had restored him to some sort of normality. 'It was one shot only – and from the harbour tower as the ships passed by. In the Pool of London they would fire a cannon to welcome an important ambassador or prince.'

'Do you think they do the same here?' Alys asked.

'Perhaps they do, but who of importance could it be? And why three such large ships? Maybe we should return to the castle with all haste.'

Shining in his eyes was a light I had not seen for many days. As he gathered his reins in his own hands and swung his horse's head towards the downward track, all memory of our adventure on the headland appeared banished from his mind.

21

The Arrival

The entire castle household was once more gathered in the great hall. This time, though, the mood was relaxed, much less tense than at the arrival of the Garter King.

I wore again my special royal livery, but I was not pushed to the front, mingling instead with a group of squires alongside the Kildare household's ladies. Alys, attired in a new light-green spring gown that was a gift from her friend Lady Kildare, spotted me and sidled through the other ladies to stand at my side. We were again close to the dais upon which Edward stood straight and tall in his spotless armour, in front of the royal standard, as before. Now he was accompanied by Lord Kildare and Sir Thomas, along with Sir Henry Bodrugan and several others of the newly arrived Yorkists.

A trumpet blared outside the enormous doors, which were then thrown open with a crash. Into the hall advanced two gentlemen, both resplendent in fine armour and colourful livery. A company of several score knights and soldiers marched in their wake. So many were crowded in, that the usually cavernous space was shrunken. The tramp of their booted feet echoed around the high ceiling of the chamber, then came an immense thunder as the men halted and stamped to attention.

One of the leading gentlemen stepped forward a further pace, then knelt down on one knee, his right hand in its steel gauntlet clamped to his heart. His companion and the company followed suit a moment later.

Lord Kildare's herald cleared his throat and bellowed, 'Your Grace, my lords, ladies and gentlemen, their lordships the Earl of Lincoln and Viscount Lovell.'

If my feelings had been taken into account, an additional name would have been announced. But I soon spotted him. Several rows back, among the other squires and gentlemen, was the cheerful freckled face of Roger de Kynton, serious for once as he played his part in this drama. Next to him, to my surprise, were other familiar faces – those of Giles Mallary and his brother Robert – the one as ever with the hint of laughter upon his face, the other closer to half a frown. But I spared little thought for them. Once I assured myself Roger had accompanied their lordships on their journey to Dublin, my attention was all for what was happening at the head of the great hall.

Edward, his face pale but composed, himself stepped forward a pace to the edge of the dais before which my lord of Lincoln knelt. As before with Sir John Wrythe, he stretched out his left hand, where the domed jewel of the regal ring glowed like a clear sky after sunset, and waited.

With no hesitation, Earl John took hold of the hand and planted a kiss upon the ring, then raised his head to look up at Edward. His broad smile was not answered on the face of the younger man.

Edward's voice was cool.

'Cousin, we greet you well – now that you have come to join us.'

From my privileged position so close to the dais, I saw the earl's smile falter. But only for an instant. Did Earl John decide in that fleeting moment to take Edward's words at face value, and not hear the criticism that could be implied? If so, his cousin's next actions showed he had made the right choice. Permitting himself a tight smile, Edward leaned forward to raise the earl to his feet with both hands before kissing him on first one, then the other cheek, as a close relation.

Earl John grasped the boy by his shoulders in response, then gave his hand a hearty shake. Their hands were still clasped as Edward directed his attention past his cousin and spoke again.

'And Lord Lovell, we are right glad to see you return safe. Rise – and all your men.'

An almighty clamour of scuffling and scraping of boots and jingling of harness broke out as the company rose again to their feet. Once quiet was restored, Lord Kildare addressed them, with his usual ready smile.

'You gentlemen are all dismissed and billets will be found for you – in the castle or in the town – somehow. 'Tis sure we were not expecting such a vast company of gentlemen today.' A laugh rang out from those assembled. Earl John bowed to his host and Edward.

'My lord, Your Grace, please forgive our coming unannounced. We travelled with all speed and did not have time to put in at a port on this coast to send a messenger to you. We dared not send ahead by sea lest the message be intercepted and – well, who knows what welcome we might have met with from the usurper's ships.'

Lord Kildare bowed in his turn.

'No matter, my lord. You are most welcome here. However you arrived. There will be lodgings for everyone – in time. Now, will your lordships accompany His Grace and myself to my private chamber? Or are you needing to ready yourselves in your own rooms before we speak together?'

'Nay, Gerald,' said Lord Francis lightly, before Earl John could respond. 'There may be too much delay before our chambers can be readied – and before we can enter them to ready ourselves also.' Lord Kildare's strong white teeth bared in a grin. 'Rather, as we have arrived with little warning, we should perhaps get on with telling His Grace our news.'

Earl John nodded in agreement.

'Then come,' said their host. 'As always the fire is burning and refreshments are set ready.'

He stood aside to allow Edward to go first, followed a step behind by Earl John, then nudged Lord Francis and nodded directly at me.

'And will you be wanting your little scribe to join us, Francis?'

His lordship glanced across to where Alys and I

stood and bowed his head to her before replying.

'I think not today. There is nothing official to record. And Edward and Lincoln are not the only ones who are being reunited here.' Hearing this, Lord Kildare threw his arm about Lord Francis's armoured shoulders and drew him through into his private chamber, talking to him like an old friend.

Relief washed through me. It had been a long day already, even though we had found a quick way down from the headland back to the city. When we had been summoned to make ready for a grand reception for important new arrivals, my heart had sunk. Discovering who the visitors were, and that Roger was among them, chased my tiredness away, but still I had dreaded being called into any formal discussions. There was only one thing I wanted to do now.

Alys must have felt the same. As the company of gentlemen and soldiers began to disperse, we both fought our way through the crowd to where we had last spied our friend.

22

'A Tangled Affair'

Months had passed since we last met Roger, back in the autumn at Gipping, yet when we came face to face again, it was as though we had never been apart.

'Roger!'

'Alys! Matt!'

He swung Alys off her feet and into a whirl, making both her skirts and happy laughter billow out around her. Then, placing her back on the ground, he embraced me. He had grown another inch or two, as he always seemed to between our rare meetings, and now stood perhaps a head taller. As we broke apart, he patted the top of my cap.

'Have you shrunk, Matt? Maybe the Irish air isn't good for you.'

Such words from anyone else would have made me bristle. But this was Roger. So I simply punched him on the arm and grinned back.

'And you – you're stretching like a beanstalk. You must be eating Lord Lincoln out of house and home. No wonder he's come to seek sanctuary with the Kildares!'

As we hugged again, Alys dropped down to her knees, making a small clicking sound with her tongue. From among the still-milling legs of the departing soldiers emerged a small white hound. It walked towards her with some timidity, then touched noses with Shadow, who stood at least a span higher.

'It's Belle, isn't it?' Alys cooed. 'I remember her from …'

A cloud passed across her face.

Roger nodded.

'You knew her the summer after little Ed … well, after Ed left us, didn't you? King Richard gave her to Earl

John then, but he says she's no use for hunting because she'd been brought up as a pet. So he gave her to me as I'd been Ed's friend. Shadow seems to remember her too.'

'She was daughter to one of Florette's early pups, I believe. I suppose that means she's Shadow's niece.'

And Murrey's too, I thought, and something stabbed me deep inside.

I bent and stretched out my hand for Belle to sniff, and then she let me fondle her soft ears. As I straightened, Roger shifted his feet as if in discomfort.

'Matt …' He hesitated. 'Matt, if you'd like to have her … I'm sure Earl John wouldn't mind.'

Heat rose in my cheeks. Had my pain been so obvious?

'Thank you, Roger.' My voice sounded gruff to my ears. 'She's yours. I couldn't —'

Alys rescued us.

'Let's pull the chairs together on the dais so we can sit and talk,' she said, hurrying to step on to the low platform. 'I doubt anyone will mind and it'll be some time before they come to make the hall ready for supper. The servants will have plenty to do, with all these new arrivals. You need to tell us what's been happening, Roger.'

We joined her on the dais and dragged the weighty seats into a rough circle – including the great carved oaken chair with its blue velvet cushion that was employed as Edward's throne.

Roger hesitated, eyeing its cavernous depths.

'Are you sure this is all right? I'm only a squire after all.'

'Don't worry. If anyone complains, I'll tell them to talk to Lady Kildare. I can do no wrong in her eyes.'

Alys settled herself in Lord Kildare's usual seat, Shadow's muzzle nestled on her lap, and Belle curled up at Roger's feet as he perched on the edge of the throne. I sat back in Lord Thomas's chair, alone.

'What on earth has been going on in England, Roger? Lord Francis left us so suddenly all those weeks ago, and all we've heard since have been rumours and gossip and little real news. What is the earl doing here? What are his plans? Where have you been?'

'Alys, Alys!' Roger held up his hands in protest, laughing again. 'One question at a time! I'll do my best to answer them – although you must remember I've not been party to everything that's been happening. I'm not sure I even know the whole story.'

'Where did you sail from? Whose great ships are those down in the Pool?' I asked. These questions had been lurking at the edge of my mind since we had watched the ships' approach from the headland.

'Ever the merchant's son, Matt?'

I blushed at his words, reminded as I had not been for some time that my family was not from among the nobility, unlike those of my friends. But neither of them noticed as Roger made himself more comfortable.

'Those questions are very easy to answer. We sailed a little over a week ago from the Low Countries, the port of Middelburg to be exact. And the ships were supplied by Duchess Margaret herself.'

'The duchess?' exclaimed Alys. 'So you have been in Mechelen. With Earl John and Lord Francis?'

'Shall I start at the beginning? Perhaps that would be easiest. Though, as I say, it's all such a tangled affair that sometimes I'm not quite sure where the beginning was.'

'How about when you left us at Gipping?' Alys suggested. 'Did Earl John get into trouble with Tudor over his little deceit?'

Roger's face was thoughtful. 'Maybe not trouble, exactly, but the king ... sorry, Tudor kept him at court, after that, very close to him. I've no idea whether he suspected he'd met Lord Francis on his visit to Suffolk – or what his spies had told him.'

'We ran into two parties of his men – well, Lord Soulsby's – at Gipping and at Lowestoft, before we could get away.'

'But you got safely back to Mechelen. We learned that, of course, from Lord Francis.'

'Then what?'

'Well, rumours came flying into Westminster from all over the place, and I suppose Tudor's spies told him things were happening in Flanders and then Dublin. So Tudor called a royal council at the palace of Sheen.'

'Was Earl John there?' asked Alys.

'Of course,' said Roger. 'Tudor may have had suspicions about him, not entirely trusted him, but he was almost his right-hand man. Along with Bishop Morton, of course, and the Stanleys.'

Alys grimaced and I suspected my features mirrored hers.

A look of sympathy flitted across Roger's face.

'Hardly the finest company, I know. And Earl John says he doesn't quite understand it himself. Although he has joked that perhaps Tudor is so insecure on his throne, he hopes a little royal-ness might rub off on him if he keeps a Plantagenet close.' He added quickly, 'I know Earl John's family name is de la Pole, but he knows his mother's family is more important. She was sister to two kings, after all, aunt to a third – and now to a queen. And some might say Earl John was the real king after King Richard died – until Tudor was anointed and crowned at least.'

'But then Tudor was foolish enough to make Edward legitimate again.'

'Was it foolish?' asked Roger. 'It means that Edward should be king, but Tudor got to marry Princess Elizabeth. That's made him king in many people's eyes.'

'Not mine,' declared Alys. 'Never mine.'

'No, nor mine, of course,' insisted Roger. 'But Matt told us that even Earl John said at Gipping that it would be difficult to justify fighting against it.'

'So what happened to change his mind?' I put in. 'When we met with him there, he was very determined not to get involved.'

'Ah,' said Roger with a knowing air, 'that was before Tudor made his big mistake.'

He cast a glance around the darkening hall, as though seeking out any who might overhear something secret. But we were alone now. Alys and I leaned closer though, to hear him better as he dropped his voice to little more than a whisper.

'We at court all knew that the prince in Mechelen with Duchess Margaret, and then in Dublin, was Edward himself. Especially when word got out that the Garter King had spoken with him and was convinced he was who he said he was. That was when Tudor and his advisers stopped saying he was claiming to be his brother Richard. They started instead to say that he claimed to be a different Edward altogether – the little Earl of Warwick.'

'How could he get away with that? Everyone knows Warwick is in prison in the Tower?'

'Well, that's when they thought they were being clever. They reckoned they could mislead everyone with false information. But I think it came back to bite them with Earl John. They said that of course the boy could not be Warwick as he was in the Tower, and then told everyone that a priest had confessed that the boy in Dublin was an impostor – only claiming to be Warwick, but definitely not him.'

Alys and I exchanged looks.

'This was a priest called Symons, or some such?'

'That's right – Symons or Simmonds,' agreed Roger. 'Well, they said he told them he'd taken some random ten-year-old boy from Oxford – the son of a baker, or maybe a tailor, no one seemed too sure – and trained him up to pass him off as a prince.'

'But why would a priest do that?'

'Or anyone?' said Alys. 'What could he hope to gain by it?'

'Well, they said it was so he could be put up by the Yorkists as a pretender to the throne. Someone to rally the people to fight against Tudor.'

'But why would this priest do that? What connections did he have with any Yorkists?'

Roger shrugged.

'I've no idea. Maybe Tudor's advisers thought they didn't need to explain it – that the people would accept anything they were told about the nefarious plots of Yorkists, no matter how strange.'

Alys's fine brows pulled together into a frown.

'Are we painted as such demons by the usurper now? Even though his own wife is from the house of York?'

'I'm not saying the people would believe it. But they might well reckon it's less dangerous not to question what Tudor's proclamations say.'

'I suppose that's possible.' She sighed. 'After all, he has punished all rebellions against him very harshly, and fined towns heavily for supporting them.'

'Anyway, this priest,' continued Roger, 'so as to pass the boy off as a prince for whatever plans he might have, had to teach him everything. From scratch, I imagine, as I don't suppose sons of tailors can always even read and write and tally numbers, let alone speak and write Latin and French, act with royal manners,' he was ticking things off on his fingers, 'know what to say and how to behave to officials and ladies, how to dance and ride and fight like a prince, and know everything about the royal family, their history and life at court … All those sorts of things that princes do.'

I reflected on all I'd had to learn in my short time at Middleham Castle. And that was just a tiny part of what Edward himself had had to study when growing up.

'That would have been impossible,' I said. 'Especially in just a year and a half since … well, since Tudor's been on the throne and Yorkists might have been planning rebellion against him.'

'Matt's right,' said Alys. 'It takes years to learn all that. Edward went to live with his uncle Rivers at Ludlow at the age of three and was still learning when his father died.'

'And Symons must have been an uncommonly learned priest to have known all those things himself,' returned Roger, with a laugh.

'And all this was achieved by a ten- or eleven-year-old son of a tradesman? Enough to persuade the Garter King of Arms that he was a prince of the realm?' Alys shook her head in disbelief.

'And that's another thing,' I protested. 'Edward's sixteen! Sir John will have clearly seen he was much older than eleven.'

'I know,' said Roger. 'But Tudor's desperate not to let people suspect that it's Edward, son of Edward the Fourth himself, who's here in Dublin. Hence trying to persuade everyone it's an eleven-year-old boy. Earl John says he's trying to keep everyone confused – mislead them with false information.'

'But it seems such a stupid idea,' said Alys. 'That a priest could pass an ordinary boy off as a prince of whatever age.

'Ah, yes,' said Roger. 'But, of course, if Earl John tries to put the truth of it out there now – that it's our Edward – no one will believe him.'

We were silent for a time. I was trying to take it all in, and from the frown still furrowing Alys's forehead, she was struggling too. Then Roger spoke again.

'Earl John said the last straw for him – after this whole daft story had been told to all the lords at Sheen – was when Tudor decided to parade little Warwick through the streets of London for all the common people to gawp at. Tudor said it was to show that the boy in Dublin must be an impostor, not the real Earl of Warwick.'

Alys gasped. 'How horrible! Poor little boy!'

'And, of course, Tudor controls all the official heralds. He's even printing proclamations so they can be put up everywhere for people to read – if they can read. So his story, and the parading of Warwick through the streets to prove he's in Tudor's hands, has been proclaimed all round the country now.'

The full truth finally dawned on me, as though his words had opened a crack that flooded my brain with light.

'So, if Edward lands in England to claim his throne, maybe no one will come to support him,' I said, each word stumbling from my mouth. 'Because they'll believe he's an eleven-year-old impostor. If they don't see him themselves, how will they know any different?'

Roger nodded. 'That's about it.'

'Well, it is a daft story,' said Alys, her eyes clouding. 'But if it does confuse everyone and stop them joining Edward, then perhaps it has been rather clever of them.'

'Well, yes and no,' said Roger. 'That's what I meant when I said it was a big mistake that came back to bite them. It made Earl John realize just what lengths Tudor would go to.' He counted on his fingers again. 'Lying and dissembling – to the lords and Parliament as well as to the people. Maybe even to Elizabeth, his wife. Exploiting little Warwick. Even trundling him through the streets like that as if he were nothing but a puppet. Well, Earl John decided he'd had enough. He and Warwick are cousins after all, and both of true royal blood.'

'Which is more than Tudor can claim for himself,' put in Alys.

'Well, yes, despite all his protests about being descended from a king of France,' said Roger. 'Anyway, Earl John decided there and then that not only would he support Edward if he landed in England, but he'd go to Flanders and offer to lead his army. So, there we went – straightaway. Along with Lord Francis, who'd just sent word to him. And here we all are now.'

'Phew!' breathed Alys. 'But what if Tudor has calculated correctly? What if people other than Earl John don't see through the lies and don't flock to join Edward? I know some have come to Dublin already, but they've all been as confused and uncertain of what's going on in

England as the rest of us.'

Roger shrugged again.

'I don't know. I imagine that's what their lordships will be discussing over the next few days – what to do next. Earl John is keen to go ahead with an invasion anyway, but I suspect Lord Francis is more cautious.'

'Perhaps Lord Kildare will sway them one way or another.'

The huge double doors to the hall opened and two servants entered, to set about lighting the brands mounted in sconces around the walls. They eyed us curiously but said nothing. Soon, I knew, more would come to make ready the trestles and benches for serving supper, so we would have to leave and prepare ourselves for the meal. Meanwhile Alys and Roger showed no signs of moving – or disturbing their slumbering hounds – so I voiced the other question that had been hurtling round my head since the Earl of Lincoln's arrival.

'That's not much of an army you've brought with you though. Three ships? How are we to launch an invasion of England with so few men?'

23

News from Home

Roger greeted my question with a laugh. Later, at supper, I was sitting close to the top table. And, above the racket made by the many other eaters, I overheard Earl John speak with all seriousness to Lady Kildare on the same subject.

'The main part of the army is still gathering with the fleet at ports along the Flanders coast, my lady. My aunt, the dowager Duchess of Burgundy, with Duke Maximilian, has been so kind as to raise and equip two thousand troops for the venture. Along with those already won to our cause by his lordship and Sir Thomas here in Ireland,' he bowed his head in recognition towards his hosts, 'we should have a sizeable force with which to face the usurper.'

Lady Kildare, who was honouring her new guests with what was now a rare appearance at supper given the imminence of her happy event, nodded graciously.

'But you and Viscount Lovell decided to come earlier – to bring your royal cousin this welcome news all the sooner?'

'Indeed, my lady. And Tudor is readying forces on England's eastern coast. So we thought it might be prudent to give him more than one place to focus on – to split his efforts. He will be uncertain where to expect our attack, if it comes.'

Lord Francis, seated a few places away, was also part of the conversation.

'We aim to keep him guessing about our true intentions, my lady. Whether we plan to invade or to build up our forces in Ireland against any action Tudor himself may take.'

'And have you decided? Whether to invade

England or remain here? If it is permitted for me to ask in such a public place as this.' She placed a hand on Earl John's arm with a winning smile. 'My husband does not discuss such things with me, so I must glean news where I can.'

A ripple of laughter ran among the gentlemen on the top table, although Lord Kildare himself did not join in. His brother, however, was grinning broadly and nudged Earl John with his elbow.

The earl remained all politeness.

'His lordship is no doubt wise not to discuss such affairs too widely. But I'm sure there are no Tudor spies within this most loyal court.' He raised his goblet to the Irish earl, who nodded at the compliment and allowed himself a smile as he returned the salute. 'I don't think there is any harm in stating we have yet to decide upon our future course of action. We have much to talk about in the days ahead.'

'But one thing that has been decided, which need be no secret, my love,' said Lord Kildare, 'is that we in Dublin shall be having the honour of crowning His Grace.'

Roger, sitting beside me, leant towards me and muttered, 'Now that's something I forgot to mention earlier. Duchess Margaret urged Earl John and Lord Francis to suggest it to Edward and the Kildares. She sent all sorts of things over with us to make sure it can be done properly.'

'A coronation?' Lady Kildare was alight with the news as she turned to Edward, in his throne-like chair beside her. 'How wonderful, Your Grace!'

Edward smiled his tight smile but said nothing. What had he thought about this sudden decision?

Lord Kildare, sitting to Edward's other side, spoke across him again to his wife.

'We're hoping it can be arranged before your confinement, my dear, so you may attend. And once the rest of the army has arrived, of course. When our king is crowned and anointed, any who follow him cannot be condemned as traitors by Tudor.'

'Will there be ambassadors from other lands?'

'Perhaps, my lady,' said Lord Francis. 'If they can be invited in good time. And if it will not make too much work for you and your household.'

'Not at all, Lord Lovell. We shall be delighted.'

Excitement flared in her ladyship's plump face.

Edward's expression was very different. An unusual flush touched his cheeks as he spoke for the first time.

'And what of my mother? We have not spoken of her. Shall she attend?'

The top table was struck quiet, although the chat and laughter continued elsewhere in the great hall. Lord Francis's cup stopped partway to his lips, while Lord Kildare turned again to spearing the meat on his platter.

Discomfort was scrawled across Earl John's face, but he took it upon himself to answer.

'Your Grace … cousin … Your mother … your mother will not be able to attend you. She has recently entered a convent.'

'A convent?' Edward let out a laugh – a sharp, unnatural sound to my ears. 'My mother? The queen? A convent?'

'Aye, Edward. Bermondsey Abbey, they say.'

'But … my mother? She is not … she has never been especially religious …'

'She has not done it of her own free will, Edward.' It was Lord Francis who spoke. 'Tudor has confiscated her lands and belongings and sent her there. She is all but imprisoned.'

The colour drained now from Edward's cheeks.

'But why?'

'We believe he suspects her of plotting with you. Or it is simply to warn her against doing so.'

'The official word, of course,' said Earl John, 'is that she has chosen to give up all her worldly possessions and retire from the world, now she is no longer queen. She will devote herself to Christ.'

'But who will believe that of my mother?'

'Very few people,' whispered Roger in my ear. Though spoken in an undertone, the laugh in the words was clear.

Earl John, though, replied in a sober manner.

'Any who wish to keep their heads, sire. It is politic to accept what Tudor says on such matters.'

'So she will not … cannot support me now?'

'No, sire. Although,' a glance travelled between the earl and Lord Francis, 'she has sent a message of support. Through your sister.'

A nudge from Roger and his breath tickled my ear again.

'That reminds me. I have a letter for Alys from Elen. Don't let me forget to give it to her.'

'My sister?' Edward's voice was bleak.

'Aye, the Lady Elizabeth,' said Lord Francis.

'Lady Elizabeth? Then Tudor still has not crowned her his queen?'

His lordship shook his head.

'She has been in touch through secret channels,' another nudge on my arm, 'and assured us that her mother – your mother – would do all that she could to help. But now, of course …'

'She can do nothing.'

'I think so. She will find it very difficult to aid us in any way. She will be watched for sure – all letters in or out read. Even if they are in code,' did his eyes flicker our way? 'that code will be broken. And, of course, such a letter would prove any suspicions Tudor has. It is maybe best not to try to contact your mother again.'

'Not, at least, until you can go to free her from her confinement yourself,' added Earl John.

If his words were meant to encourage Edward, they were not perhaps a success.

'When our invasion succeeds?'

'Aye, cousin.'

'If, in fact, we choose to invade.'

'Indeed, if we so choose,' said Lord Francis, then hesitated. 'Or rather, if you so choose.'

'But now is not the time to discuss such things,' declared Earl John. 'Perhaps tomorrow, in council ...'

Those around him nodded their agreement.

Edward looked from one to another. Then, as though taking the hint and changing the subject, he said, with a vague air,

'I met a lady today,'

'A lady, Your Grace?' returned Lady Kildare, a smile touching her lips. 'One of our young ladies here in the castle?'

Her eyes sought out Alys at the far end of the high table, beyond the reach of the conversation. Had Lord Francis told her ladyship of his suspicions – perhaps to alert her before he went away earlier in the year?

Edward did not see her glance. Emptiness crept into his eyes.

'Nay, she was not young. And perhaps few would call her a lady.'

Concern rose in me at what he would say. But I could not attract his attention, to distract him – not from here. I felt Roger lean forward as though to hear better against the noise in the rest of the great hall.

'She said – or seemed to claim – that she knew my grandfather.'

'The old Duke of York?'

'She called him a fine man and a friend of Ireland.'

'Such he was.' Lord Kildare raised his cup again in salute. 'Your Grace's grandsire was a good man and an able and just governor of our land. He was the rightful king and his sons reclaimed the throne for those of his blood. I and my family shall help his grandson do the same, if God wills it.'

'I thank you, my lord.' Edward bowed his head to him. 'But ... but the lady had a warning for me.'

'A warning?'

At Lord Kildare's sharp enquiry, some of the squires at our table looked up in surprise. But with the arrival of servants bearing platters of fruit and cheese, they soon lost interest.

Roger, though, raised his eyebrows at me as we both strove to hear. Alys and I had told him a little of the day's adventure, but had been shooed out of the hall before we could give much detail.

'Yes, my lord,' Edward continued. 'It appeared to be a warning. She told me my grandfather had sailed away over the sea and become king of nowhere. She told me not to make the same mistake.'

The gentlemen at the top table were silent. It was Lady Kildare who spoke again.

'And where was this … this lady, Your Grace?'

'Upon the headland overlooking the bay. I rode that way with my friends for exercise.'

Her ladyship shot a look Alys's way again, then shook her head at her husband, who had opened his mouth as if to speak. He promptly closed it again.

'Was she living alone up there, Your Grace?' Lady Kildare asked, placing her hand on Edward's arm. His fingers were clenched about the handle of his knife, though I had seen him neither cut nor eat anything for some time.

'Aye, I believe so.'

'There are many such hereabouts,' her ladyship said in a soothing tone. 'Both men and women. Hermits of a sort, seeking to be alone. If they're not mad at first, they soon become so. Think not on what she may have said.'

'But she recognized me as king.'

'You are very like your father, they say, Your Grace.'

'But it was my grandfather she spoke of.' Edward was gazing now at Lady Kildare like a child seeking reassurance from its mother. 'My grandfather. Who set out from Ireland to claim his throne – and failed.'

'Perhaps she saw him once when he was governor, long ago,' she said. 'It gives her no authority to speak, or special foreknowledge of your quest. Think no more on the ravings of a mad person.'

She reached across to the platter of fruit now set before him and picked out a piece.

'Come now. Taste one of these tiny oranges. They were brought to us by their lordships from the merchants of the Low Countries. They grow in the furthest reaches of Spain, they say, and are sweet beyond honey. And they may be eaten without the use of a knife to cut them,' she added, gently lifting his fingers from his knife and placing the round bright fruit within them.

Edward surrendered his knife without protest. Tearing the skin from the fruit, he eased its tiny segments apart and placed them between his lips, one by one, chewing in silence.

Relieved, the gentlemen about him resumed their conversation, with Sir Thomas's raucous laugh soon ringing out again above the general hubbub of the room.

Edward took no further part in it. I watched him as he sat staring out over the throng of the household, no expression on his face.

24

The Letter

For all Lady Kildare's efforts, the desolation in Edward's eyes remained as we all gathered in his chamber after supper. He had pleaded tiredness to his hosts and their guests as he retired, but my friends and I he had summoned with a glance.

As we entered, he was slumped in his chair before the fire. Another tray of the tiny oranges was set upon the table before him, reflecting the flickering gold of the flames. But Alys had had the presence of mind to collect both her hound and Roger's before we joined him. In a few minutes their tail-wagging excitement at new-found friends had worked its intended magic.

'They're so alike,' he laughed, fending off Shadow as Belle gathered herself for another attempt to leap on his lap. 'If Belle were not so much smaller, I couldn't tell them apart. Are they from the same litter?'

As Alys explained the hounds' relationship, memories of Shadow gambolling like this with her sister Murrey flooded back. The usual pain washed through me, and I cast my thoughts around in an effort to distract myself. I remembered Roger's aside at supper.

'You said you had a letter for Alys, Roger.'

'Did I?' Roger's eyebrows rose in surprise, as Alys's chatter faltered to a halt.

My voice had come out louder than I expected.

'Have you, Roger?' Alys asked him, although her eyes flicked across to me. Edward appeared not to notice, his attention all on ruffling the fur on the dogs' heads, while also reaching into his pouch for tidbits.

'Oh, yes,' recalled Roger, fishing in his own purse. He pulled out a small square of parchment, sealed with a blob of red wax, and handed to Alys. 'From Elen.

She gave it to me when last we met in London. In case we should travel to join you.'

Alys broke the seal with deft fingers and unfolded the letter. A shadow swept across her face.

'But it's in code. Why —? How —?'

'Why is easily answered,' said Roger. 'Tudor is suspicious of everyone. He has spies everywhere. Did you not hear what was said at supper?'

'Very little,' Alys retorted. 'I was not so close to the action as you two. Young Master FitzGerald would keep talking to me of some falcon Earl John had brought to his uncle as a gift from the duchess. Much as I love hawking, I would rather have heard more of what their lordships had to say.'

'Never mind that now,' Roger said, airily. 'We can fill you in later. What has Elen to say? I've been carrying that letter for weeks. Are you not amazed that I was never tempted to open and read it?'

Alys glared at him.

'Not really. You knew it could not be urgent or very important, or she would have told you to your face.' The cloud returned to her own face now. 'But I cannot read it. And that answers the "how". Elen will have found my copy of our code amongst the things I left behind when I fled from Gipping.'

'But I have my copy.'

I rummaged in my pouch. My fingers brushed against the cool hardness of coins, the soft leather binding of a small book, sundry scraps of paper and parchment, before closing on a tiny scroll fastened with a silken ribbon.

Roger laughed as I drew it forth.

'You keep it close to you at all times then.'

My cheeks flamed at his words, but as she took the cipher from me, Alys said coolly, 'Matthew, at least, has always taken his oath seriously.'

'His oath?'

Edward's voice broke into our three-way

squabble. He sat forward now in his chair, one hand resting on Belle's head, his eyes alight with interest.

Roger fidgeted, glancing first at me, then Alys. But she was pushing aside jug and goblets on the table to make room to spread out the letter and the scroll, side by side.

I smiled encouragement at Roger, as I stepped across to pour wine into cups for us all. With both of us turning away, he was compelled to answer the question on our behalf.

'Well, Edward,' he began. 'Well, many years ago at Middleham, when I was still just a page – and Matt was too, of course …'

As he told Edward, with obvious embarrassment, the story of how we had come to form the Order of the White Boar, I handed round the drinks, then joined Alys at the table.

She was trying to hold the scroll flat with one hand, while she traced the lines of Elen's letter with a finger of the other, picking up a pen from time to time to record the deciphered words on a third piece of parchment. So far all she had scratched in her untidy handwriting were the words 'Dear Alys, I hope this letter reaches you …'

But the letter was many times the length of that short sentence, crammed in on every square inch of the unfolded parchment in Elen's neat but tiny handwriting. If Alys's lettering resembled the death throes of a spider half-drowned in an ink well, Elen's would not have been out of place in York Minster's scriptorium.

'Let me help,' I said, lifting her hand from the scroll. 'You tell me the letters, I'll work out what they stand for, and you write them down. What day did Elen write the letter?'

'It was a Thursday.'

Her look at me was full of gratitude before she bent over her task again, spelling out each coded word as she ran her finger across it.

'D L Q P W J.'

'Safely,' I said quietly and she jotted it down. And so we worked on.

By the time Roger had finished his story, we had decoded more than half the letter. Much of the first part was enquiries after our health and laments that we were apart, but then came a change.

'What does she have to say, this old friend of yours?'

So absorbed was I in deciphering the letter that I flinched, startled by Edward's raised voice. But Alys just stared across the table at him as though her thoughts were miles away.

'Does she write much of what's happening in London?'

Alys chewed a moment on her lip before she answered.

'Not really, Edward. But she does have a message for you.'

He started up towards us, dislodging both hounds from their comfortable resting places.

'A message? For me? What message?'

Alys's eyes flashed towards me as she held up a hand to stop him leaning closer.

'We still have to decode it. It may take a little time yet – and patience.'

But patience was not a virtue Edward possessed in abundance. He began to pace around the room, from time to time peering over Alys's shoulder.

'You should have got Matt to do the writing,' he said, squinting down at her scrawl on the paper. 'He has a fine hand. I can hardly make out the first words of yours.'

She swivelled to face him and arched an eyebrow.

'Then wait until we have finished, and I shall read it out to you.'

Chastened by her look and tart tone, he retreated to his chair. With Roger, he spent the next few minutes bribing the hounds to sit, and beg, and offer their paws for a flurry of tidbits. At that instant I felt I too had received a treat from his hand. Those were perhaps the first words of praise of me he had ever uttered. Yet I wished they had been for a more important, or even just useful, service.

Before too long, Alys and I had completed our task. She grasped her goblet, downed a prodigious gulp of wine, smiled a tight smile at me, then swung round to Edward.

He leapt to his feet.

'Is it done?'

'Yes, Edward, it is.'

He pulled up a chair by the fire and waved her to it.

'And? What does she say? The message.'

With a deliberate movement Alys sat down, arranging her skirts with care. I refilled her goblet and set it upon a nearby table, then retired to stand behind her.

'Come, Alys. The message.'

Edward seated himself too, but this time perched upon the edge of his chair, leaning forward, eagerness shining in his eyes. After a quick glance at Alys, Roger enticed the hounds away to a stool in a corner, where he settled them at his feet, out of the way.

Alys smoothed out the scrap of paper covered with her scribbles and cleared her throat.

'Elen says she is back in London with Lady Tyrell – or at least she was when she wrote the letter. And she says they were both summoned to court by … by your sister, the Lady Elizabeth. She says Elizabeth is still not queen – or still was not then.'

Edward's face darkened, suddenly stormy.

'Still not? As Lord Francis said at supper. This Tudor has no respect for her – or for her family. He marries her, but …'

He left the words hanging. Was he angrier at the marriage, or at Tudor's failure to crown Elizabeth? Or perhaps at his own powerlessness?

Alys's eyes slid askance at me, then down to the parchment again.

'Elen says Elizabeth took her aside to speak to her in private and asked her to pass on these words, if she could, to her brother. She said, "He must not think me unhappy. My life has not turned out as I would have wished – my husband is not the man I hoped to wed. But he has not treated me ill. And I have my beautiful son, Arthur. He is my life now. But tell my brother I will support him whatever he decides. Whatever destiny he seeks. I will await his decision – and so will our mother. Send our love to him."'

Alys didn't look up as she finished reading. She folded the square and placed it on the table, before picking up her wine cup.

A moment of heavy silence passed. Then,

'Her beautiful son?' Edward's words, spiked with bitterness, speared through the quietness. 'But he's Tudor's!'

Alys said nothing.

Roger stooped to stroke Belle's head, waking her out of her sleep.

If neither would speak, then I —

'He's just a baby, Edward – just a few months old. He can't help who his father is.'

Edward stared at me, emotions chasing one another across his eyes, like tempest-driven clouds. As he opened his mouth, no doubt to lash out at me, Alys plunged in first.

'Matt's right, Edward – you know he is. Whatever his father has done. And Elizabeth – she's still your sister.'

She carried on talking, reminding him of what else the Lady Elizabeth had said – about her support, her love.

I was thankful for being rescued. As she spoke, and Edward's thundery face cooled, my memory was torn back to my own sisters, at home in York. One had been little more than a baby herself when last I saw her – and there was also the baby brother I had never yet seen. Richard my father and new mother had named him, after our king, my master. He would be two, almost three years old now – walking, talking, getting up to mischief.

The images swam before my mind's eye. Yet I had no idea how either child fared – or the rest of my family. We had been unable to exchange letters for almost two years, so afraid was I that they would fall into the wrong hands. Were my family well? Did they even all still live?

A pang of homesickness wrenched at me. To distract myself, I thrust my attention back to the others. They were engrossed in their conversation. Even Edward, who was calmer now. No one had observed my distress.

Roger was saying, 'Do you think Lord Francis was right at supper? That Tudor would be able to break our code if he got hold of one of our letters? If I had been caught and Elen's letter taken from me?'

Alys sipped at her drink, her eyes pensive.

'I suppose so. After all, don't forget, we chose a simple code on purpose so little Ed could use it.'

Worry slipped across Roger's face, but in a moment cleared.

'But it won't matter any longer – not now we're all together. We won't need to use it again.'

'Except Elen,' I said – rather loudly, for a second time that evening.

Alys raised an eyebrow.

'Why would she need to write to us again? Soon we'll all be in England.' Her eyes darted at Edward, before she said quickly, 'Perhaps.'

Edward's face was expressionless once more as he sat, now well back, in his great chair. Perhaps sensing his earlier emotion, Shadow had padded over to him and her pale muzzle rested upon his knee. He caressed the tuft on her head in an absent manner as he said, with some hesitation,

'Yes. Perhaps. Their lordships and I have much to speak of in the coming days. Whether to stay here where I am acknowledged king, and maybe lure Tudor to us, or – or go to England to reclaim my throne.'

Alys bowed her head to him, but I could see her bite her lip.

Roger didn't pick up on the change of mood.

'Anyway, even if we do go to England, you won't be with us, Alys.'

She rounded on him, her awkwardness fled.

'Why not?'

'Well ...' he stuttered, caught by the whiplash of her words. 'Well, it will be an invasion. We'll be going to fight. An army.'

'Why should that stop me?'

She was on her feet now. Both hounds, disturbed by her abrupt movement, sprang up too, Shadow sidling against her skirts, a tiny grumble growing in her throat.

'But ... but you're a girl!'

'There are often girls and women with armies,' Alys countered. 'Campfollowers. Who do you think does the cooking for the men?'

The flare of the fire glinted in her green eyes. Why didn't Roger back down?

But of course, they had known each other for the longest time. He just laughed.

'But they're ordinary girls and women. Not ... not ladies.'

Alys snorted.

'Being a lady has never stopped me before.'

'That's true,' said Roger, with his usual lazy grin.

'Nor will it this time.' Edward cut into their quarrel. 'You are as fearless as any man I've met, Alys. If you wish to travel with the army, you shall.'

Roger sobered up at his resolute tone.

'Lord Francis and Earl John will not like it.' He hesitated, but then ploughed on. 'Nor, in truth, do I.'

He was right about their lordships. And I didn't like it either, for all my wish to be longer in Alys's company. After all, I had seen the reality of an army on the march.

But Edward drew himself up straighter in his

206

chair, his face imperious.

'Who is king?'

Neither Roger nor I had an answer to that, of course.

As we kept our silence, Alys's eyes blazed her triumph. She turned her most dazzling smile on Edward.

'Perhaps I should dress as a boy again – as I did before, at Gipping. Lady Kildare can help me this time. If you truly don't mind me coming?'

He nodded to her, a smile brightening his own face for the first time that evening.

'It would please me very much.'

Roger glanced at me, with the faintest shake of his head. His eyes were shadowed with puzzlement.

I thought back to what Lord Francis had said to me all those months ago in Mechelen, when we'd spoken of Alys travelling to Dublin.

'If you are determined to do this, Alys, I think we must keep it our secret,' I said, my voice as light as I could make it. 'Especially from Lord Francis.'

25

Conspiracy

Lord Francis was so busy over the coming days that he had no time to detect our little conspiracy. In fact, the whole castle was a-flurry with frantic activity as preparations got underway for Edward's coronation.

Lord Kildare's chamberlain was in charge of the arrangements, working closely with Lord Francis and Earl John to ensure all was done in the correct manner. Both of those gentlemen had of course taken part in another such ceremony only four years before, so were well placed to offer their expertise. Lord Francis's usual air of seriousness if anything hung heavier about him during this time, the furrow on his brow only deepening as each day passed. Of all our elders and betters at the castle, only Lady Kildare appeared unperturbed. She was, as Alys said, awaiting her own important event, with a calmness that contrasted with the busyness of all those about her.

'What is a simple confirmation of a king,' her ladyship had said to her, 'compared with bringing a new life into the world?'

'I suppose she's right,' said Roger, but with uncertainty clouding his voice. 'After all, a lying-in is a difficult and dangerous time for a lady.'

Alys just laughed.

'It's her sixth confinement, Roger. It's dangerous, yes, but mostly she's frustrated not to be involved in the arrangements. Lord Kildare won't let her, because of her delicate condition. He doesn't wish her to exert herself.'

'Then it's lucky you have given her such an easy task to occupy her, away from all the hustle and bustle.'

Edward's words had drawn from Alys a smile rivalling the glitter of sunlight on a tumbling summer stream. My own and Roger's feelings on the matter were very different. We had seen Alys and Lady Kildare together start work upon that task, two or three days before.

Alys had been standing, laughing, in the older lady's private chamber as two maid servants fussed about her. They were busy transforming her into a boy as her other protector, Lady Tyrell, had also done almost two years before at Gipping. Then she had been disguised to escape our enemies – this time it was to evade the notice of friends.

The maids had already helped pull on hose and undershirt, before Alys had insisted Roger and I be admitted. She wanted us to witness her transformation. Soon she was also adorned with a jerkin, rough shoes and a cloak fit only for a servant in the castle's stableyard.

We had hung back, uncertain. Lady Kildare, resting heavily upon a cushioned bench, watched all with a critical eye, her hands folded on her swollen stomach. As Alys twisted all about to give both herself and us the best view of her new attire, her ladyship said shortly,

'Your hair, my dear.'

Alys's fingers had sidled to the reddish tendrils that, as ever, had slipped from her lacy coif. She grasped the flimsy fabric and tore it away. The curls, released from their netted prison, framed her face, making her look far younger than her years. No grown lady, young or old, would be seen with their hair loose like this.

'You must cut it,' she said.

Lady Kildare shook her head. 'Not I.'

'It's been cut before.'

'So I see.'

Her ladyship's dainty nose wrinkled. She pushed herself up from her seat and lumbered towards Alys, raising one hand to touch the wayward curls, her other delving into her huswife pouch.

'Perhaps, as it's so short already – with a few pins – here … and here …' She deftly coiled and pinned several strands up and out of the way. 'There. Maybe we can hide it under a kern's cap. It will not be for so very long after all.'

Alys held still under her ministrations, but a firmness stole into her eyes.

'But it must be for good, my lady. For all the time I am with the army. Lord Francis must not recognize me at any time, or he will leave me.'

'Leave you, my dear? Not once you are a-sail, or have landed safely in England.'

'That's when I shall be in most danger.'

'Nay.' Lady Kildare laughed. 'Not danger, surely. Not if you do as you have promised me and stay well away from any battle that may occur.'

But Alys's face was sombre.

'Danger, indeed, my lady. Lord Francis, if he found me – or Earl John, also – would leave me at the very first house of an ally we came to. And make me promise to stay far away from their march. And that I would have to do – if I promised. And then … if word somehow reached Dame Grey … then I am lost.'

'Dame Grey?'

'Aye. I am her ward, don't forget. And she would have me marry —'

Alys's mouth twisted rather than utter the name.

Lady Kildare hardly seemed to notice.

'Her ward? But … but you know the dowager queen has entered a convent? And that all her possessions have been seized … well … officially…'

Her words trailed off in their turn.

It was only then I recalled Alys had not heard all that was said at the welcome feast. And she had no idea of how cruel a blow she had been dealt by events in faraway England. The cruel blow even I had recognized only later that evening, after Roger and I had retired to the chamber we now shared. We had discussed Alys's predicament long into that night – and had both been such cowards we had never spoken of it to her.

I felt him now, close beside me, tense, as he said,

'The official word is that she has donated everything to the king ... that is, to Henry Tudor.'

'What?' Alys rounded on him. Despite her violence, Lady Kildare's pins did their job well – no tresses shook loose. But the meaning of Roger's words, and the violence done to her by it, had shaken her at once.

'Everything? You mean ... you mean, Tudor is my — that usurper is my guardian?'

Roger nodded.

Horror splashed across Alys's face. She whirled round to stare at Lady Kildare.

'Is this true?'

Her ladyship plucked at the rough sleeve of Alys's jerkin.

'It is, my dear. I know I said I would help you in this deceit, but ... are you sure you would not rather stay here with me?'

Something flashed in Alys's eyes – anger, defiance? Not despair.

'When Edward has claimed his throne, my lady, I'll return to you then – in triumph.' She placed her palm on the immense swell of Lady Kildare's belly. 'And we will see this little one – who will grow up under the rule of a good Yorkist king.'

A good Yorkist king? I might question the wisdom of Edward letting Alys accompany him to England, but I had no doubt he would prove a good king. With his cousin and Lord Francis to advise him, he promised to be a worthy heir to his father and his uncle.

During those late spring days he spent much time in conference with the earl and Lord Francis, as well as the Kildare brothers and many other experienced counsellors. And he took time, amidst all the coronation frenzy, to consider, discuss again, and reach his own conclusions as to his future plans. He even, as often before, used me as a sounding board.

As ever, I was not expected to express an opinion. That was the role of his trusted, older advisers. I was only

211

to listen and, on occasion, nod in agreement.

'Two thousand troops will arrive soon, Matthew,' he told me one day. 'Sent by my Aunt Margaret to serve me. Their captain will be Martin Schwartz. He's a renowned warrior, veteran of many campaigns in Flanders. The men he will bring are the fiercest German soldiers – equipped with arquebuses and pikes. And word keeps coming from England – from allies there. Friends of my father, my cousin, Lord Francis. Good men. They too will lead great companies of men to support me if I land in England – or join us here.'

I nodded. I too was aware of all the news, but repetition of it to me reinforced it for him.

'And then there are the allies I have made here in Ireland – through Lord Kildare's good offices. His brother Thomas will himself lead their contingent.

I nodded again. Sir Thomas would be a welcome addition to any party – not just for his skill in arms, but for his jovial company. He had often cheered Edward during our stay, when he was beset by doubts or unhappy at some news.

'And they say Tudor quakes in his boots at the thought of anyone marching against him,' Edward continued. 'Each revolt or plot against him so far has made him more cautious, more fearful of those around him. Lord Francis's attempt on his life at York last year may have failed, but it helped our cause. He knows the country is not behind him, that many will rise against him if I invade. And my cousin Lincoln's flight to join us has made him more wary still. He doesn't trust even those close to him. That must be why he has shut up my mother – his own wife's mother – in a convent too.'

But then he paused, his eyes shadowed.

'Yet this may all forewarn and forearm him. He will be well prepared to meet us if we do invade. We know he has spies everywhere, waiting and watching, and spreads lies among the people to try to turn them against us. If we decide to invade, we must take care where and when we land – keep him guessing as long as we can.'

Another moment of silence.

'It is not an easy decision to make, Matthew. Should we stay here and force him to come to Ireland to face us – or should we grasp our courage with both hands, place our trust in God and take ship for England? What would my father have done?'

That was a question I could not answer – even had he wished me to. Old King Edward. He had often been rash and acted in an ill-advised manner. And as he grew older, he left his fighting to others – such as his brother Richard. Yet in his youth he had been bold. And his daring actions had won him his crown, and later regained it for him when all appeared lost. Much in this Edward reminded me and others of his father – but was it enough?

'John and Francis say I must decide for myself – that they cannot settle it for me. They are right, of course, and I know they will both support me whatever I choose.' He sighed. 'It is so hard to be king, Matthew. And as well as all this, I must prepare for my coronation. It is a sacred act, and my duty to do it well. My head spins with all that I must think on.'

And I was transported back to one of our first meetings. All of four years before. When I rode with him from Stony Stratford to Northampton and heard his lament about all that was happening then. The death of his father, the loss of his uncle and brother. And having been thrust into the kingship so young. My heart had gone out to him then, at twelve years of age, and it did now too. Once more, I did not envy him and his position. Let alone the decision he must now make.

But make it he did, at last. And the day before his coronation, the whole city knew he had made it – and knew this young king would remain among them no longer. He would soon set sail for England to reclaim his throne.

26

No Longer King in Waiting

The day of the coronation dawned clear and bright.

I woke early. Soft fingers of sunlight were slinking through the window of my antechamber and playing warm across my cheek. I had barely slept at all until the later watches of the night, knowing what the coming day was to bring.

I roused myself, plashed water from the waiting basin upon my face and hurriedly dressed before knocking and entering Edward's chamber.

Had he too perhaps had little rest? He did not say, but sat already in the window recess, clad in undershirt and hose, gazing out upon the early bustle in the courtyard. The morning sun splashed gold upon his tousled hair and the paleness of his face as he turned to me.

'My stomach churns, Matthew,' he said by way of greeting. 'As it did when we were upon the sea all those months ago. Yet I do not find that the castle has transformed overnight into an ark upon a tossing sea. Nor that an earthquake has occurred and set the ground to trembling. The grooms and servants out there,' he gestured through the stone mullions, 'seem to be about their business as usual. If a little busier perhaps.'

He sent another look towards me as I lingered in the doorway. The shadow of a smile slipped across his lips and was gone. At that moment he reminded me more of his uncle Richard than he ever had before.

A tremor ran through me at the memories stirred, but I shrugged them aside, lifting up my hands, full of the platter of bread and cheese and jug of watered wine I had collected on my way.

'Will you break your fast before your body

servants come to dress you?'

'Nay. I think that would be tempting fate – or tempting my quaking stomach to betray me.'

'The food may help settle it.'

He shook his head.

'I would rather keep my insides and my head clear today – the day I truly become king.'

And indeed, he bore himself like a true king all day. From his robing in the rich velvet and cloth of gold garments his aunt had sent from Burgundy. Through the solemn procession along streets lined with cheering crowds of men, women and children stretching from the castle to the grey bulk of Christ Church Cathedral, crouched like a sleeping lion in the midst of the tangle of city streets. To the rituals of anointing and crowning within the cathedral's cavernous depths, and the joyous celebrations that came after – when at last he could relax and enjoy the day and the feasting and entertainments it brought.

I and my friends were honoured with a place in the royal procession, loyal servants of the new king and his lords as we were. My own view of it was perhaps not so clear as that of the last coronation parade I had seen – that of my lamented master King Richard in Westminster less than four years before. Then I had watched from the sidelines, my mouth agape at the finery on display, at the beauty of the gowns and banners, the richness of the regalia – of crowns, sceptres, gem-encrusted swords – and overwhelmed by the tremendous blasts of the trumpets, the heralds' cries, the crowds' cheers and hurrahs. But to be in the midst of it as we were on this day, as the procession wound through the hordes of excited onlookers – rather than being such an onlooker myself – was an experience I would not have missed for all the riches in the world.

Far ahead of us, I could glimpse the colossal gilt crucifix catching the fire of the morning sunshine as it was carried high above the city's archbishop. He led the royal company, pacing sedately among a gaggle of sumptuously clad fellow bishops, abbots and priors.

Just behind them I knew followed a dozen or more noblemen, all bearing symbols of kingship. Though I could not now see them, as we had assembled in the castle courtyard in Sir Thomas's hands were a pair of gilded spurs, in those of his brother Lord Kildare the enormous sword of state presented to the city by the usurper Henry Bolingbroke many years before, while Lord Francis hefted a magnificent staff of silver gilt.

Earl John strode in the special place of honour just in front of his cousin Edward. He held, on a purple velvet cushion, an ancient golden crown, finely wrought but simple in design. It was a holy crown, taken I knew, for this momentous day alone, from a venerable statue of the blessed Mary, mother of Christ, that resided in a church near the city's Dame's Gate.

Next came Edward, walking the whole way to the cathedral barefoot, as I remembered my old master and his queen had done, to display humility before God.

When he entered the great cathedral, still some way before us, a cacophony of trumpet blasts, choir song, organ music and more cheers erupted, sweeping back towards my friends and I as we approached the wide steps up to the carved-stone doorway. We soon passed through after him into the ancient, pillared nave. We winced at the clamour that smote our ears and blinked at the candlelight twinkling from every side and glancing off the silver, gold and bright-hued silks adorning the people crowded inside. Rainbows of sunlight streamed down from the tall coloured-glass windows, and incense drifted upwards towards them, like early morning mist.

The shattering sounds of cheers and fanfares faded only as Edward stepped up to the high altar. There stood the archbishop, resplendent in his gold-embroidered robes. Beside him was the carved and gilded bishop's chair where the new king would soon be enthroned.

As my young master knelt before the symbols of

our Lord, the archbishop called upon him to swear his coronation oath, and upon those of us present to bear witness to it.

I stood alongside Roger, both attending Alys, who was seated now amongst the ladies of the Kildare and other lordly households. Together we heard Edward swear his oath in English, as his uncle had before him. He pledged to uphold the laws, customs and godly peace for the people of England and Ireland, and to exercise justice with mercy in all his judgements.

His voice never faltered as he recited the words used from time immemorial by all kings of England. Had the love flowing from those people who thronged the streets to acclaim him king banished the nervousness that had gnawed at him?

Next came the anointing with holy oil, screened from our view by the churchmen and lords now clustered about Edward, and soon the sunlight filtering through the arched windows gleamed upon the ancient crown as it was raised high above his head. The archbishop solemnly intoned the sacred rite, while those around him echoed the venerable Latin words.

A moment of stillness.

Then the crown was lowered upon Edward's head, and at last he was truly king.

The cathedral exploded in song, fanfare, music and shouts of acclamation, and the bells in the tower high above rang out the joy in all our hearts.

And in that instant I was whisked back to my perch outside the abbey of Westminster as that earlier coronation reached its climax. When I was a thirteen-year-old apprentice forging a fresh life in London, as a new era under a new king began, and a world of possibilities was born. When I had no idea what my future would bring – no notion of the turmoil of the coming rebellion, the death of my little friend Ed and then of his mother. When far from my mind were the devastation of battle and the loss of my old master, my flight with my friends and Edward and young Richard, my exile abroad, and no contact with my family for almost two long years.

And the torment of emotions rising within me almost choked me, rooting me to the spot, as all those about me surged forward to greet their new king.

I saw Edward rise to his feet and pace past us the long length of the aisle towards the west door.

I saw the crown nestling upon his fair hair, the silver-gilt sceptre clasped in his left hand, and a real smile upon his lips for the first time that day.

I saw Alys and Roger mingling with the crowds of lords, ladies and churchmen who fell in behind him, cheering and applauding.

And as I craned to see past the throng, my eyes following Edward as he led them from the church, I caught sight of Lord Francis, standing apart, in the shadow of a pillar.

His face was expressionless, but the knuckles of his hand gripping the pommel of his sheathed sword were white with strain. Was he recalling, too, that earlier coronation in which he had also played a part – the crowning and anointing of his great friend and liege lord, King Richard? And did he, too, remember where the road that began that joyous day had led?

But before I could ponder more on the matter, the tide of people swept me forward, along the aisle, alongside Alys and Roger, washing us all out into the brilliant spring sunshine.

And there we were witness to Edward the Fifth, son of Edward the Fourth, his face now wreathed in relaxed smiles, raising his arms and his sparkling sceptre to the cheering crowds gathered in the square before the cathedral.

The roar in response deafened me. I could see Alys's laughter, but not hear its music. Roger's mouth opened in speech, but no words reached my ears. All about us was thunderous as a summer storm, or as cannon on a battlefield, and above our heads the bells pealed in riotous celebration.

And I knew Edward was no longer king in waiting, but true king. Not only here in Ireland, but also of our beloved England.

And we were going home.

Here ends KING IN WAITING, the third book in the sequence called THE ORDER OF THE WHITE BOAR, following the second book THE KING'S MAN. The fourth book, SONS OF YORK, will relate Matthew and his friends' continuing adventures.

Author's note

Many years ago, when I went for my first interview for a place at university, the eminent professor in whose presence I sat, terrified, asked me what was the essence of archaeology. Through his subsequent questions, he guided a trembling, hesitating eighteen-year-old to the realization that it was interpretation. Any historian would no doubt agree, as likely would any historical novelist. Certain 'facts' may be known (perhaps dates, places, names or artefacts), but it is interpretation that makes the (hi)story.

In terms of the story I tell in *King in Waiting*, I stick to the 'facts' that we know – ones that are agreed on by various records close to the time of their occurrence. For example, Viscount Francis Lovell spent time in sanctuary in Colchester after the fateful summer of 1485; rebellions against Henry Tudor frequently occurred throughout the English lands through 1485–6 and beyond; Margaret, dowager Duchess of Burgundy lent her support to someone who was crowned King of England in Dublin in May 1487 by the city's archbishop with many lords attending, including John, Earl of Lincoln and Lord Lovell himself.

But who that person was who gained such support is less clear. The sources of the time conflict. Was it a boy or a young man? Who was it he claimed to be – the young Earl of Warwick or a son of King Edward IV, either the younger, Richard of Shrewsbury, or the elder, Edward, formerly Edward V? And was he genuinely who he claimed to be or an impostor?

It was only in the years following 1487 that a full (hi)story of these events evolved, and it was a story that suited the first Tudor king, who was still sitting uneasily on his throne. And it's this story that has largely been accepted over the past five centuries. After all, as they say, the winners write the history – and the Tudors were certainly the winners for more than a century after the battle that became known as Bosworth.

But I have preferred to return to the scant 'facts' that we know of the events of 1486–7 and to provide my own interpretation of them, as I did in the previous books in this sequence, *The Order of the White Boar* and *The King's Man*.

And if you've read those books and this far, you'll know who the king crowned in Dublin is in my (hi)story.

Many (if not most) people think Edward Plantagenet, the eldest son of Edward IV – who was set aside as king in 1483 when his father's bigamy was proclaimed – died in that year, probably at his uncle King Richard III's hand. That's because this is what later Tudor writers (and most famously William Shakespeare) said. But delving back into the records of the decades immediately after Richard's death in battle reveals many other possibilities – and many discrepancies, irregularities, contradictions and outright holes in that 'official' story.

The plain truth is that all we can say about the two sons of Edward IV, who later became known as 'the Princes in the Tower', is that they were not *officially* seen *in public* after the summer of 1483. Perhaps King Richard himself didn't know what happened to them. It certainly appears Henry Tudor didn't. If the 'official' (hi)story is correct, then surely, after he became king, he would have explicitly recorded their deaths by murder and accused Richard of responsibility. He never did – and neither did his wife (their sister) or their mother – over more than two decades.

Maybe one day we will find out. Perhaps it will be revealed by the 'Missing Princes Project' directed by Philippa Langley (who was part of the team responsible for finding Richard III's grave). In the meantime, all is speculation and interpretation of the 'facts' we know – whether in non-fiction histories or my own work. *King in Waiting* and its soon-to-be-published sequel, *Sons of York*, are my contribution to the ongoing thread of debate about the events of 1486–7.

There is perhaps more speculation here than in my previous books, mainly because far fewer records still exist relating to the events – and most of them are contradictory and/or written well after those events took place. So I have continued the story as set up at the end of *The King's Man* and have taken it forward in what appears to me to be the most logical way. Perhaps it may encourage you to reconsider 'official histories' and the value of interpretation generally. But mostly I hope you enjoy the books as fiction, albeit based on 'facts'!

About the author

A Ricardian since a teenager, and following stints as an archaeologist and in publishing, Alex now lives and works in King Richard III's own country, not far from his beloved York and Middleham.

The discovery of Richard's grave in 2012 prompted Alex to write *The Order of the White Boar* and its sequel *The King's Man* to bring the story of the real man to younger readers. *King in Waiting* and its sequel *Sons of York* explore his legacy in the following years.

Alex has also edited two anthologies of short stories by authors inspired by King Richard III: *Grant Me the Carving of My Name* and *Right Trusty and Well Beloved...*, both sold to raise money for Scoliosis Association UK (SAUK), which supports people with the same condition as the king.

Alex has also published a standalone book, *Time out of Time*, following the timeslip adventures of Allie Turner who discovers a doorway into the history of an ancient English house, Priory Farm.

The fourth book in the *White Boar* sequence will be published in 2022 under the title *Sons of York.*

Follow Alex on social media at:

Website:	alexmarchantblog.wordpress.com
Amazon:	www.amazon.co.uk/Alex-Marchant/ e/B075JJKX8W/
Facebook:	www.facebook.com/AlexMarchantAuthor/
Twitter:	twitter.com/AlexMarchant84
GoodReads:	www.goodreads.com/author/show/ 17175168.Alex_Marchant
Instagram:	www.instagram.com/alexmarchantauthor/

Elen's letter to Alys

The full text of Elen's letter to Alys from London found in the chapter 'The Letter' reads as follows. If you wish to decipher it for yourself, the code of the Order of the White Boar can be found at the beginning of the book, after 'Cast of Characters'.

Oplc Lwjd

T szap estd wpeepb cplnspd jzf dlqpwj. T htww rtgp
tee z Czrpc ld sp dljd sp xlj eclgpw ez jzf lrlty.

Lcp jzf lyo Xleesph hpww? Wzco Pohlco lyo
Wzco Qclyntd ezz? T szap hp dslww xppe lrlty dzzy.
T xtdd jzf lyo zfc wtqp ezrpespc.

T lx ty Wzyozy yzh htes Wloj Ejcpww lyo
slgp dppy Dtxzy. Sp dljd Xldepc Nliezy ecpled stx
hpww - lyo Xlee xfde yze mp ezz pygtzfd!

Wlde hppv, Wloj Ejcpww lyo T hpcp dfxxzypo
ez nzfce mj Wloj Pwtklmpes. (Dsp td detww yze
bfppy.) Ty actglep, dsp ldvpo xp, tq T nzfwo, ez
epww spc mczespa:

'Sp xfde yze estyv xp fyslaaj. Xj wtqe td yze
ld T htdspo - xj sfdmlyo td yze esp xly T szapo ez
hpo. Mfe T slgp xj mplfetqfw dzy, Lcesfc. Sp td xj
wtqp yzh. Mfe epww xj mczespa, T htww dfaazce stx
hslepgpc sp opntopd· Hslepgpc opdetyj sp dppvd. T
htww lhlte std opntdtzy - lyo dz htww zfc xzespc.
Dpyo zfc wzgp ex stx.'

Lyo T dpyo xtyp ez jzf. Delj dlqp, Lwjd, lyo
nzxp mlnv ez fd dzzy.

Pgpc jzfc qctpyo,

Pwpy

Also by Alex Marchant

Time out of Time

Welcome to the golden summer of 1976. Year of the Heatwave, year of the Drought.

Normally sun-starved and grey, England is plagued by endless blue skies – no rain for months, the country scorched and parched, standpipes in the street.

But 12-year-old Allie has other worries. When her family moves to ancient, ramshackle Priory Farm – far away from her friends and everything she has ever known…

Then she discovers a doorway into history – and her adventures begin. What secrets will Priory Farm reveal?

An exciting timeslip adventure by the author of *The Order of the White Boar* sequence, *Time out of Time* whisks the reader off to explore one small part of England through the ages – with some explosive moments in time…

Available from Amazon, all good bookshops or direct from Alex: AlexMarchant84@gmail.com

The Order of the White Boar

How well do you know the story of King Richard III? Not as well as Matthew Wansford.

Matthew, a 12-year-old merchant's son, has always longed to be a knight. And his chance comes in the golden summer of 1482 when he arrives at Middleham Castle, home of King Edward IV's brother, Richard, Duke of Gloucester – valiant warrior, loyal brother, loving father, good master.

Soon Matt encounters a dangerous enemy. Hugh, a fellow page, is a better swordsman, horseman, more skilled in all the knightly arts – and the son of an executed traitor. A vicious bully, he aims to make Matt's life hell.

Yet Matt also finds the most steadfast of friends – Alys, Roger and Edward, the Duke's only son. Together they forge a secret knightly fellowship, the Order of the White Boar, and swear an oath of lifelong loyalty – to each other and to their good lord, Duke Richard.

But these are not times to play at war. Soon Matt and his friends will be plunged into the deadly games of the Wars of the Roses. Will their loyalty be tested as the storm looms on the horizon?

For readers of 10 and above.

'A really gripping historical novel . . . well written, vivid and absorbing.' E. Flanagan, author of *Eden Summer*

The King's Man

How well do you know the story of King Richard III?

It's April 1483, and the death of his brother King Edward IV has turned the life of Richard, Duke of Gloucester upside down, and with it that of his 13-year-old page Matthew Wansford.

Banished from Middleham Castle and his friends, Matt must make a new life for himself alone in London. But danger and intrigue lie in wait on the road as he rides south with Duke Richard to meet the new boy king, Edward V – and new challenges and old enemies confront them in the city.

As the Year of the Three Kings unfolds – and plots, rebellions, rumours, death and battles come fast one upon the other – Matt must decide where his loyalties lie.

What will the future bring for him, his friends and his much-loved master? And can Matt and the Order of the White Boar heed their King's call on the day of his greatest need?

The King's Man, the eagerly awaited sequel to *The Order of the White Boar*, continues the story of Richard Plantagenet for readers aged 10 and above.

'A book full of action, heart, fire and hope. A cracking read, and I highly recommend it.' Narrelle M. Harris, author of *Kitty & Cadaver*

Grant Me the Carving of My Name

With a Foreword by Philippa Gregory

&

Right Trusty and Well Beloved...

With a Foreword by Philippa Langley

Two anthologies of short fiction by authors inspired by King Richard III, sold in support of Scoliosis Association UK (SAUK)

'I want you to tell my real story... Use any talent you have to show me in my true light, not painted black with Tudor propaganda. My new army must be wordsmiths, not soldiers; artists, not knights; musicians, not warriors. We will lay siege to the towers of Tudor lies and bring them crashing down...'

Who, for you, is the real Richard III?

Is it the boy, exiled in fear to the Continent aged seven? The loyal warrior, brother to Edward IV? The young man struck by tragedy? The just and rightful king? Or Thomas More's and Shakespeare's infamous villain?

You can meet them all within these pages ... or can you?

'An inspired idea.'

'A mixture of the serious and the light-hearted, this anthology of Ricardian short stories is a must read.'

Printed in Great Britain
by Amazon

66505937R00135